HIGH STAKES DECEPTION

VANISHING RANCH
BOOK 6

CHRISTY BARRITT

CHAPTER
ONE

AS AINSLEY TATUM sat in her car staring across the street at Carter Winslow's stately brick home, she considered backing out of this assignment. Leaving. Pleading conflict of interest.

But if she'd been able to bring down cartel members when she was a Texas Ranger, then she was certainly capable of facing the man who had broken her heart all those years ago.

She glanced up and down the sunbathed Denver, Colorado, street as the stakes of this assignment slammed into the forefront of her mind.

Carter's father, Doyle, had been killed in a suspicious car accident almost a year ago. Ainsley didn't believe it was an accident.

In fact, she and her team at Vanishing Ranch had been investigating a terrorist bombing in Florida from fifteen years ago—a bombing that had killed her brother, Jason, who'd been interning for a US senator at the time.

They'd found a trail of US citizens connected with the event. Their evidence indicated that someone powerful—or a group of powerful people—had planned the event and framed international terrorists in order to cover their tracks.

Their working theory was that Doyle had discovered the involvement of several people he'd done business with. When these men learned Doyle knew too much, he'd been permanently silenced.

Ainsley and Carter needed to uncover the truth without raising suspicions. They would pose as newlyweds in order to meet with one of those men under the guise of exploring a business proposition.

Ainsley's nerves thrummed inside her at the thought.

So much was on the line right now—and she wasn't even talking about her heart.

However, she had to get moving. Jack Earl, her number one suspect, was expecting Carter this evening. She didn't want to be late and miss any opportunities.

As she reached for the handle of her SUV, Carter's front door opened.

She paused and watched as a beautiful woman

stepped onto his porch.

Ainsley's gaze darkened.

Of *course*.

Even though she and Carter were supposed to be newlyweds, he'd still found time to entertain another woman—and possibly blow their cover in the process. What if Jack had men watching them? Didn't Carter know they needed to be careful?

The woman with him now looked like just his type. Tall and slender with dark hair, refined features, and an impeccable taste in clothing.

So maybe Ainsley wasn't *totally* over what happened between them.

But that was silly. She was a grown woman. She should be able to put the past behind her.

Carter certainly had.

With that sobering thought, Ainsley kept watching.

Carter stepped outside behind the woman. Handsome, handsome Carter with his tousled blond hair, striking blue eyes, and broad shoulders. The man was both handsome and brilliant. He'd developed software that cut back online identity theft by fifty percent.

Two years ago, he'd sold his company, and Ainsley's understanding was that he no longer had to work. Yet he was still involved in the tech field, using his intelligence as a private contractor on whatever projects he chose.

Ainsley watched as Carter and the woman laughed together. Then he leaned toward her, kissed her cheek, and the woman turned to leave. Her high heels clicked on the immaculate shrub-lined sidewalk as she made her way to a BMW parked in the driveway.

Ainsley released a long, pent-up breath.

She should just call her boss, Charlie Soldier. Tell her that she needed to find someone else for this assignment.

In fact, that's what Ainsley would do. She didn't have to put herself through this emotional turmoil. She didn't have anything to prove.

She grabbed her phone from her purse, ready to make the call.

Before she dialed any numbers, she looked up once more and watched as the woman opened her car door and climbed inside.

As Ainsley's fingers hovered over Charlie's number, an explosion filled the air.

Carter heard the blast. Saw the flames. Felt the heat gust across his face.

He watched in horror as fire consumed Maureen's car.

No . . .

"Maureen!"

She'd just climbed inside. Maybe it wasn't too late to get her out.

He prayed that was the case.

Shielding his face with his arm, Carter darted toward her vehicle.

Reaching it, he tried to grab the handle.

The heat was nearly unbearable.

As the flames seemed to shrink for a moment, he saw his opportunity.

He grabbed the handle in one last attempt to save her.

Heat blistered his skin, and he jerked his hand back.

The flames were too high, too intense. The fire engulfed the entire vehicle.

He couldn't even see Maureen through the flames.

But he couldn't just stand there!

He started to reach for the door again when someone jerked him back.

"You can't save her!" a high-pitched voice shouted. "It's too late."

As the horror of what was happening washed

over him again, he couldn't tear his gaze away from the car. He had to do something!

He started to reach for the door again.

Before he touched it, the person beside him rammed her shoulder against his abdomen.

Tackled him to the ground.

As his body collided with his grassy lawn, another explosion ripped through the air.

The gas tank, he realized. The flames had reached the gas tank, causing another blast.

Carter sat up and ran a hand over his face, hardly able to comprehend what had just happened.

"Maureen . . ." he muttered.

This couldn't be possible.

The heat from the blaze scorched his skin as sirens sounded in the distance.

His gaze remained on the burning car as the truth settled into his chest.

Maureen couldn't have possibly survived that.

"Carter . . . I'm sorry," a soft voice said.

A voice that sounded familiar.

A voice that instantly swept him back to the past.

He glanced beside him, and the air left his lungs when he saw the figure staring at him.

"Ainsley?" He choked out the word.

He hadn't seen her in years. *Years.*

But he'd thought about her often.

Too often.

If possible, Ainsley Tatum looked better today than she had sixteen years ago. She'd always been tall and thin, but now curves graced her body in all the right areas. Her straight, honey-blonde hair and smattering of freckles gave her a wholesome girl-next-door look.

But her eyes weren't nearly as innocent as they'd once been.

No, they were filled with experience. Grief. Maybe even pain and regret.

Ainsley stood, wiped the grass from her jeans, and then she helped him to his feet. "The police are on their way. We don't have much time."

He stared at Maureen's car again as the fire continued to burn.

An ache panged in his chest.

"I'm sorry about your loss," Ainsley continued. "But it's too late to rescue her. Your friend is gone. The blast killed her immediately."

Carter knew that. But he didn't want to accept it as the truth.

He rubbed the skin between his eyes, hardly able to process the scene before him. He'd just been chatting with Maureen. Telling her about how he truly believed there was a time for everything and a season for every activity.

He hadn't expected to be confronted with her death so quickly after the proclamation.

Ainsley grabbed Carter's arm and shifted him until he faced her. Then she locked her gaze with his, clearly trying to drive home a point.

"Listen, Carter," she started. "If we're going to sell our story, we need to start pretending. Now. As far as anyone is concerned, you and I just got married."

His mind blanked as he tried to comprehend what she was saying. "What?"

"Come on . . ." She tilted her head. "Charlie went over all this with you."

He squinted, still in a state of shock. "Charlie? Charlie Soldier?"

Ainsley stared at him another moment as if he'd lost his mind. "Yes. Of course, I'm talking about *that* Charlie."

He raked a hand through his hair, not caring if he left it standing on end. He needed to shake off his shock and try to focus.

Was that even possible?

He pressed his eyes closed as he thought through the situation. "Wait . . . *you're* the one Charlie sent from Vanishing Ranch? You and I are supposed to pretend to be married?"

What kind of joke was this? Everything about it

was a terrible idea. *Terrible*.

Confusion raced through Ainsley's gaze. "I thought Charlie told you."

"Charlie only told me she was sending one of her operatives. She didn't give me a name. Doesn't she know that you and I," Carter wagged his finger back and forth between them, struggling to find the right words, before he finally finished with, "have a past?"

Ainsley planted her hands on her hips as she stared up at him. "I told her. But she insisted on sending me. She said we're both professionals. When the police get here, we're going to tell them we just got back from a month-long trip to Mexico where we met each other and spontaneously eloped. Got it?"

Carter's eyes widened, but he nodded.

That would be a little easier considering the fact he truly had just gotten back from Mexico. No doubt, Ainsley knew that.

Having Ainsley help him find the truth threw a whole different spin on the situation.

They were supposed to act like newlyweds.

Him. Ainsley.

What were the odds?

He eyed her again, thankful for the distraction from the burning car. Maybe.

But there was still a lot he didn't understand.

"I thought you were a Texas Ranger," he finally said.

"I was. I'm not anymore."

Carter wasn't sure what to think of this.

Things hadn't ended well between them. Ainsley had refused to listen when Carter tried to explain his side of the story. It probably wouldn't have mattered what he told her—she wouldn't have believed him. She'd been too angry.

Maybe he deserved that. The situation had been complicated, to say the least.

As two cop cars squealed onto the scene, Ainsley thrust something into his hand. "Wear this."

His breath caught when he looked down and saw a wedding ring.

Quickly, he slipped it on. Glancing at Ainsley's hand, he saw she already wore one.

Their charade was now official.

Carter glanced back at Maureen's car one more time.

His heart thudded with grief as he tried to process this loss.

Was Maureen's death somehow connected with his father's death? With Jack Earl?

Determination hardened inside him.

Carter would figure it out if it was the last thing he did.

CHAPTER
TWO

AINSLEY STARED at the man who'd introduced himself as Detective Geoff Jamison. He was in his fifties and on the shorter side. The hair he lacked on top of his head he made up for with his shaggy eyebrows and mustache.

He'd taken her and Carter's statements as firefighters put out the flames and paramedics examined what remained of Maureen. Police officers had stretched crime-scene tape around the area, and neighbors gawked out their windows.

Knowing she needed to put on a show, Ainsley slipped her arm around Carter's waist as the two of them stood on the front lawn. She had to pretend to be a supportive spouse comforting her grieving husband.

But just touching Carter made her want to run.

At one time, she'd enjoyed nothing more than the feel of his strong chest beneath her fingertips. Seeing the warmth in his gaze. Dreaming about what a future with him would be like.

But getting attached to him was one of the biggest mistakes Ainsley had ever made.

She wouldn't let that happen again.

Still, she reminded herself that Maureen could have been someone very special to Carter. He seemed truly grieved over what had happened.

This wasn't part of the assignment. Ainsley was only supposed to come here, pick Carter up, and drive nearly four hours from his home in Denver to the luxurious resort where they'd be staying in Aspen, Colorado.

The drive would give them plenty of time to get their story straight.

But now, all that had been turned upside down.

And she had a bone to pick with Charlie. Why hadn't her boss told Carter that Ainsley was the one who'd be coming? Charlie wasn't the type to over-look a detail like that.

She'd withheld that information from Carter on purpose.

"How did you know Ms. Langston?" Jamison asked Carter.

"She is—she *was*—my lawyer." Carter rubbed his

throat as if it pained him to say the words. "She stopped by so we could finalize a contract. I had to sign some paperwork."

"What time did she arrive?"

"She was probably only at my house for thirty minutes before . . . this happened."

Jamison's gaze wandered to the house where two cameras were visible. "Do you have security footage? We need to see if anyone tampered with her car."

"Of course. Whatever you need to find out who did this to her." He paused. "This wasn't an accident."

Detective Jamison raised his shaggy eyebrows. "I'm inclined to agree. Cars usually don't just explode on their own. Is there any reason why someone would have wanted to hurt Ms. Langston?"

Carter shook his head, grief suturing his gaze. "None that I know."

Something about his heartache made Ainsley's heart pang with compassion. She didn't want to feel sorry for Carter. Not after what he'd done to her.

Yet she couldn't look at a grieving man and not feel empathy. Carter had just suffered a shocking loss. This situation would be a lot for anyone to handle.

Still, Ainsley was counting the minutes until she

could remove her arm from around Carter and put some space between the two of them.

"Let's get inside and look at that video." Detective Jamison nodded toward the front door.

Ainsley's heart pounded harder.

She hoped the footage might provide some answers.

Carter's father had already died.

Now Maureen.

And fifteen years ago, Jason, Ainsley's brother and Carter's best friend, had been killed.

Probably by Jack Earl, the man they were to meet with.

Her jaw hardened with resolve.

She didn't want anyone else to be added to that list.

———

Carter still couldn't believe that Ainsley was here beside him.

That Maureen was dead.

That he was about to embark on a charade that could totally ruin him and his family's name.

Or that could redeem it.

He didn't care anymore. He'd checked off all the goals he'd wanted to accomplish in life. He'd reached the success he'd craved and the status and wealth that came along with it.

But in the end, it was all meaningless, just like King Solomon had said.

Now, all Carter wanted was justice. He lived and breathed that desire.

Felt it growing to the edge of vengeance.

He always reined it back in. Always prayed for wisdom. Always hoped he was strong enough to heed the difference between justice and revenge.

Right now was no different.

He brought Detective Jamison into his office, where the two of them sat behind the desk. As Carter brought up the footage on his computer, he glanced over at the stunning Ainsley Tatum as she lingered near the door.

The time he'd spent with Ainsley that one summer during college had been some of the best days of his life.

Then his bad decisions had reared their ugly heads.

Their time together had ended.

Too quickly.

Too messily.

To this day, Carter still regretted what had happened. Still regretted he hadn't fought harder to explain the situation to Ainsley. Regretted that he'd allowed himself to be swept up in other people's expectations.

"What do you think?"

Carter realized Detective Jamison had been talking to him. He ran a hand over his face and looked at the screen.

"I'm sorry," Carter muttered. "I still can't get over what just happened. My head is spinning."

"It's understandable. I'd like to see the footage from the time Ms. Langston pulled up until the explosion."

Ainsley crossed the room and stood behind Carter, resting her hands on his shoulders.

Electricity raced through him at her touch.

She still had that effect on him, even after all these years. That could be a problem.

Carter knew Ainsley was standing close and touching him only so she could also see the security footage. What better excuse than to appear as if she were a new spouse trying to comfort her husband?

Her fingers gently kneaded the tight muscles at his neck and shoulders.

He wanted to lean into her, to give in to the relaxation she offered.

But he couldn't do that.

Because none of this was real.

Except for Maureen's death.

Grief twisted his heart again. Maureen was a long-time family friend who'd been there for him after his father's death. She'd always tried to look out for him.

Now she was gone.

Carter forced himself to concentrate on the video in front of him. He found the moment Maureen pulled into the driveway.

Then they all watched.

No one touched the car from the time Maureen arrived until the time she climbed back in and started the engine.

He also watched as Ainsley stopped at the curb across the street. She'd sat in her car for several minutes, not getting out until after the explosion.

That was a coincidence . . . right?

Ainsley stopped massaging his shoulders and rested her hands on his back instead. He sensed her gaze was riveted to the screen also.

"Where were you arriving from?" Detective Jamison turned to Ainsley. "If you don't mind me asking?"

"No, of course not. As you may or may not know, Carter and I just got married. We met down in Mexico and eloped."

On a whim, Carter took her hands and led her in

front of him. He pulled her into his lap and wrapped his arms around her waist.

They might as well play this up.

He *did* get a small amount of satisfaction when he saw the flash of surprise in her gaze—an emotion that quickly disappeared as Ainsley slipped back into character.

"Since our wedding was so spontaneous, we're still trying to work out some of the logistics," Ainsley continued. "But the two of us are taking off to Aspen today, so I grabbed a few things at my old place then came here."

Jamison raised his eyebrows again. "You didn't see anything suspicious when you pulled up?"

"I didn't. I knew Carter and Maureen were meeting, so I stayed in my car to give them a few minutes. Besides, I had some text messages I needed to respond to."

"My best guess is that someone put this bomb in Ms. Langston's car earlier, and they were waiting for the right moment to trigger the detonator." Detective Jamison's gaze met with Carter's. "Whoever did this had to be close for the signal to work. My guys are searching the neighborhood now, but the perpetrator is probably long gone."

The pit in Carter's stomach grew deeper.

Ainsley wrapped an arm around his neck and

frowned. "I'm so sorry, baby. I just can't believe this . . . I never met Maureen, but you spoke so highly of her."

Carter didn't know what to say. But he did have to wonder . . . what if Ainsley had been the one to detonate the bomb? She'd been close enough to activate it and smart enough to pull it off.

But . . . why would she do something like that?

That's what he wasn't sure about.

In his line of work in the tech field, he'd learned not to trust too easily. Learned that people who were supposed to be on his side sometimes weren't. The more successful he had become, the more people wanted to use him, to exploit him.

As he glanced at Ainsley again, nausea pooled in his gut.

It was always best if he remained on guard. To never fully trust. To be suspicious.

Even when he didn't want to be.

CHAPTER
THREE

AINSLEY SAW the distrust in Carter's gaze as he glanced at her.

She couldn't blame him.

She knew how this situation looked. She'd pulled up and sat in her SUV while looking at the house. A few minutes later, Maureen's car exploded.

Did someone want to set Ainsley up? To cast suspicion on her?

Her gut twisted at the thought.

If that was true, then that meant someone was keeping an eye on Carter. Maybe on her.

That would make this whole scheme even more complicated.

But the whole situation was cutthroat. This wasn't an amateur's game.

No, the people they were investigating were the

best at what they did—manipulating, misaligning, and doing whatever it took to get exactly what they wanted.

"Do you mind if we look in your SUV?" Detective Jamison asked Ainsley.

"Not at all."

The vehicle was in her name, and there wasn't anything inside other than her luggage. She and her team had covered all the bases, just in case. Being undercover required careful attention to all the details.

She reached into her purse then handed him the keys, carefully avoiding her gun. "Here you go."

The SUV wasn't a problem—but the gun in her purse could be. If Detective Jamison asked to look through it, he'd find the weapon. He'd ask questions.

Even though Ainsley had her concealed carry permit, she knew the weapon might raise his suspicions.

As the detective disappeared from the room, Ainsley jumped from Carter's lap and scowled.

Carter rose to his feet, standing mere inches away. "What? Aren't we supposed to look like we're in love?"

She heard a touch of resentment in his voice.

Ainsley wanted to argue with him, but she

couldn't. Carter was right. That was *exactly* what they were supposed to be doing.

They had to make this relationship look real. It was the only way they'd find the answers they needed. Too many suspicions would be raised if Carter showed up with anyone else other than a spouse.

The people who knew Carter well knew he wouldn't come to this kind of event with someone who was only a girlfriend.

That's why the two of them needed to make this relationship look real.

Ainsley needed to use her law enforcement background to watch his back. To ask probing questions. To get a read on the entire situation.

She glanced at her watch. "Jack is expecting you today. You don't have much time to waste."

"We can't leave until the detective clears us." Carter moved closer and lowered his voice. "Do you think Jack is behind this? Do you think he killed Maureen?"

"I have no idea. Did your dad know Maureen?"

"She was his lawyer also."

Ainsley didn't like the sound of that, but she tried to keep her face placid. "Do you have any other enemies?"

"I have a lot of enemies." His jaw tightened as he

lifted his head. "People who wanted me to sell my company to them. Who were upset when I didn't. However, I don't know any who'd want to kill Maureen."

"Maybe she had her own list of adversaries. She was a lawyer."

"It's possible." Carter frowned. "But I can't believe this timing is a coincidence. Why now? Why at my house?"

"You're right. The timing and location were most likely deliberate." Ainsley glanced out the window at the scene outside. "Let's just see what the detective says next. But the stakes just became even more deadly."

His frown deepened. "Yes, they did."

Thirty minutes later, Detective Jamison cleared Carter and Ainsley to leave.

Carter had given the detective a copy of the security camera footage as well as his phone number in case the investigator needed anything else.

In the meantime, cops were scouring the area for anyone suspicious. Jamison would talk to Maureen's next of kin—her brother if Carter remembered correctly. She'd never been married and didn't have any children.

He'd talk to her coworkers and friends. Try to trace her path this morning to figure out when someone could have tampered with her car.

But, right now, there was nothing else Carter could do for Maureen except mourn.

Carter knew it was time to go. However, he was leaving one hard situation and heading into another. Adding more stress was the fact he had to pretend Ainsley was his wife.

The woman was one of the bravest people he'd ever met. She'd been one of the few women bull riders. Most women in rodeo did barrel racing or roping.

But she hadn't let being a woman in a sport dominated by men slow her down.

When Carter had seen her at the rodeo riding those bulls, he'd never experienced anything like it. He could have watched her for hours—even though he'd worried about her at the same time.

She'd even won some titles.

Ainsley had been fascinating, especially to Carter, who was a certified city slicker.

In college, he'd become friends with Ainsley's brother, Jason, and had come to work at their family ranch for a summer.

That's when Carter had met Ainsley, and his entire life had been turned upside down.

In the best possible way.

Until the best possible way ended and only heartache remained.

"Are you ready to go?" Ainsley's voice pulled him from his thoughts.

Carter jerked his mind back to the present. "Let me just grab my bags."

He dreaded this whole charade. But he had to find out answers. Innocent people had died at the hands of someone who felt untouchable.

He feared they might be planning something else.

But Carter knew he couldn't find answers or stop them by simply sitting on the sidelines. He had to immerse himself in the game—even if it cost him everything.

He returned downstairs a few minutes later and met Ainsley. As soon as they stepped out the front door, he took her hand, reminding himself that they needed to put on a show.

The gesture would be good practice for when they met Jack Earl, the CEO of NorthStar Media, the world's largest social platform. The man also had his hand in several other businesses and served on numerous advisory panels for the government.

The brilliant man was worth billions. In fact, he'd

become somewhat of a celebrity over the years. He had that personality—one that easily put him in the spotlight. He'd even been photographed with world leaders from across the globe.

With one more wave to the detective, Carter and Ainsley walked toward her SUV.

She'd insisted on driving. Maybe it was better that way.

Carter's hands still had a slight tremor after witnessing the explosion.

The good news was that Ainsley's SUV hadn't been out of anyone's sight since she'd arrived. Detective Jamison said they had checked it over, just to be safe.

That made Carter feel a little better.

Until Ainsley suddenly jerked to a stop beside him.

Carter paused and studied Ainsley's face, wondering what was wrong.

Then his gaze followed hers, stopping on the yellow rose on her windshield.

WHERE DID that rose come from? Carter wondered.

He glanced beside him. "Ainsley?"

She seemed to snap from her thoughts as she turned toward him.

"I . . ." She opened her mouth and closed it again as if unable to form the right words. Without answering him, she looked around at the first responders near them. "Did anyone see who left this rose here?"

They all shook their heads and continued working.

"Ainsley? What's going on?" Carter tilted his head, still waiting for an explanation.

She glanced around one more time before

plucking the rose from the windshield and staring at it.

Clearly, there was a story here. But maybe this wasn't the time or place to talk about it.

Besides . . . how had someone been able to leave that rose on Ainsley's car without anyone noticing?

It didn't make sense.

"Everything okay?" Detective Jamison appeared behind them, his eyes narrowed with inquisitiveness.

Ainsley held out the flower, a knot of confusion on her brow. "I found this on my windshield. It couldn't have been there for long."

"You're right. It wasn't there when we searched your car." Jamison grunted and scanned the area around them before his gaze darkened. "Looks like we need to take another look at that security footage."

Carter pulled the video up on his phone. This wouldn't be as clear as his computer, but it would be faster.

When he stared at the images, he realized an ambulance blocked the sight of Ainsley's SUV.

"Curious . . ." The detective turned back to Ainsley. "Is there any significance to the flower?"

"I . . . I don't think so." Ainsley's nose twitched—although just barely.

It was her tell. What she did when she wasn't stating the complete truth.

But what was she covering up?

Suspicions tightened Carter's spine even more.

Jamison nodded slowly. "We'll keep this as evidence and look into it."

"Is the SUV still safe to drive?" Ainsley asked.

Jamison nodded. "It would have only taken someone a few seconds to leave this rose. Planting a bomb would take much longer. You should be good to go."

Relief swept across her features as she smiled and thanked the detective.

But as soon as Jamison stepped away, the smile slipped from Ainsley's face.

Carter didn't know what to think right now.

Could he trust Ainsley?

He wasn't sure—and that uncertainty didn't make him feel better.

Without saying anything else, Ainsley opened the back of her SUV, and Carter placed his bags beside her luggage.

He didn't know what this weekend would hold.

He could walk away with answers.

He could walk away with more questions.

Or he might not walk away at all.

Ainsley stood near her SUV and glanced at the scene around her once more.

She did *not* like how this assignment was starting.

Not at all.

A yellow rose hadn't been left for her in two years.

Had Dante found her again? Was he back? Out of prison early?

A sick feeling swirled in her gut.

"Ainsley?" Carter's voice pulled her from her thoughts.

She glanced at him as he stood on the other side of the SUV. Questions glimmered in his gaze as he stared at her.

She swallowed hard. Not now. She couldn't explain this situation here.

Carter was supposed to be in Aspen in six hours. They couldn't afford to miss that meeting. Their entire assignment hinged on spending time with Jack Earl.

Ainsley simply had to pretend for three days and two nights that she and Carter were married.

Then she could be done with this and resume life as normal at Vanishing Ranch down in Arizona.

But, instead of moving, Ainsley scanned everything around them again.

That familiar, merciless feeling nagged at her.

The feeling she was being watched.

She rubbed her tightening throat.

"Are you ready to go?" Carter's voice snapped Ainsley from her thoughts.

She turned back to him and reminded herself to get a grip. "Let's hit the road."

But as she climbed inside her SUV, she sensed danger was closer than ever. Waiting around every corner.

Maybe even right beside her.

CHAPTER
FIVE

AINSLEY'S MIND continued to race.

She knew she owed Carter an explanation.

But she waited until they were on their way through the Colorado mountains before she started. "A few years ago, someone . . . someone dangerous . . . began leaving me yellow roses."

"What does that mean?" Carter narrowed his eyes. "Someone? You don't know who?"

Ainsley had to hand it to him—at least he didn't beat around the bush. She could appreciate that.

"It's nothing that you need to concern yourself with," she said.

"It's a little late for that." Carter folded his arms across his broad chest. "My friend is dead. Immediately after she dies, you get a mysterious yellow rose. Despite a lot of people milling around, no one saw who left it. Plus, you're acting weird." He paused. "My life is in your hands this weekend, Ainsley. If you want me to trust you, then you need to share more than that."

"Point taken." Ainsley wanted to argue, but she couldn't. She would feel the same way. She let out a long breath. "A couple of years ago, I had a stalker. He left roses for me—among other things."

Carter's eyebrows flicked up in surprise. "Do you think this guy is back? Now?"

"He should be in prison." She stared out the windshield as the road snaked around a mountain.

Carter gave her a lingering look as if he didn't know what to think about that statement.

Ainsley let out another long breath. "Look . . . I can tell you more about it later. Right now, we don't have a lot of time to get our cover story straight. We're going to need to do that before we get to Aspen if we're going to sell ourselves as a couple."

"Very well." Carter's jaw flexed. "What would you like to know about me since we last spoke sixteen years ago?"

———

Carter didn't like the fact that Ainsley was keeping secrets. He didn't like the fact that trouble was chasing her.

They already had enough things to be concerned about.

Charlie Soldier's whole plan was turning out to be a bad idea.

He'd heard of the woman before she'd sought him out a month ago with her proposal.

Charlie had risen to fame through tragedy after her football star father had left his prestigious career in order to join the military. Her dad—Benjamin Soldier—had lost his mom during the Florida hotel bombing.

The same bombing where Jason had been killed.

Afterward, Benjamin Soldier had given up everything—ultimately, in every sense of the word.

He'd become a hero and icon to many when he walked away from the NFL to join the military and fight the terrorists responsible for the bombing. While doing so, he was killed during an overseas operation.

But Charlie was convinced there was more to her father's death than met the eye. She believed he discovered information on the bombing and was permanently silenced. She'd spent countless funds and resources to find out what.

That had led her to Jack Earl, a computer genius who was known for his backroom deals and powerful connections. Several board members from Jack's company had been at the hotel during the bombing. A few had been gone when the explosion happened. When Charlie had talked to one of those board members, a man named Everett Maurice, he'd reluctantly opened up.

He'd told her about a hard drive Jack often traveled with—a hard drive where supposed company secrets were kept. But Everett thought there was more to the story. He told her that Jack hired outside contractors—security contractors—who did some kind of clandestine work for him.

When Charlie had discovered that Jack was trying to persuade Carter to work for him, she'd contacted Carter. Together, they'd come up with this plan to meet Jack, become friendly, and hopefully find this hard drive.

But she'd insisted Carter couldn't go at this alone. That he needed backup in case things went south. That he needed someone—a trained agent—to watch his back.

And now, here he and Ainsley were.

Carter knew that the car accident that claimed his dad's life wasn't truly an accident, no matter what investigators had said.

Someone had killed his dad.

His bets were on Jack.

Carter just needed to find out more information. He needed more answers.

He needed justice for his father.

At the thought, his hands fisted with determination.

"Before we talk details, I need to know about Maureen," Ainsley said as she gripped the steering wheel. "Why would she have been killed? Was she working with you on something?"

"Like I told the detective, we were just finalizing some contract stuff."

"I need to be blunt with you." Ainsley stole a glance his way. "Did you have any romantic interest in her? I saw the kiss on the porch, so I have to ask."

He scowled. "No, I'm not dating anyone. She was just a good friend."

"I'm sorry for your loss." She paused. "When you say, 'some contract stuff,' what does that mean?"

He shrugged, not wanting to get into the details. Privacy on the matter was important to him for multiple reasons. "It's nothing important. Nothing that should tie in with this."

"But someone was clearly following Maureen. Most likely, this person knew you worked with her and wanted to send a message."

Maureen had died because of him . . . that was a hard truth to stomach.

Carter stretched his neck as tension threaded his muscles. "I suppose that makes the most sense. But I can't imagine why anyone would target her. There are many other people I'm closer to."

Ainsley frowned. "I don't like the way this whole thing has started."

Carter crossed his arms. "Believe me. I don't either."

———

Ainsley swallowed hard as her thoughts raced.

"I hate to ask this, but what if someone is already onto us?" Carter's question hung in the air.

"I thought about that also, but I don't see how that's possible," Ainsley said. "My tech team has worked it all out. They even photoshopped pictures of us, making it look like we've been together over the past few weeks."

"The only person I've talked to about this is Charlie."

"And she's always careful. Maybe this is all because someone doesn't want you to meet with Jack Earl."

"Or maybe this has to do with the person who left

that rose."

Heaviness hung in the air between them for a moment.

Finally, Ainsley spoke. "We'll have to keep our eyes wide open until we figure this out. In the meantime, the two of us met while vacationing at a resort in Mexico. We fell in love, extended our stay, and decided to elope."

"Love at first sight, huh?" Carter's voice sounded strained.

"That's right." Ainsley kept her eyes on the road in front of her, not liking the thoughts racing through her head. Thoughts about how when she and Carter had first met, she *had* fallen head over heels in a matter of days.

What a mistake.

You could never truly know someone in such a short amount of time. Ainsley had learned that the hard way.

"If anyone asks what you do for a living . . . ?" Carter asked.

"I'm the marketing manager for a car dealership in Phoenix. The job sounds boring enough that people shouldn't ask too many questions."

"Okay." He stared out the window also. "We're going to Aspen. Can you ski?"

"I can if I absolutely have to. But I prefer hot

climates and horses to snowy mountains and slippery pieces of wood attached to my feet any day."

A slight smile curved his lips. "You never did like the cold, did you?"

The way he said that made it sound like he'd never forgotten her.

Or their time together.

The thought sent a strange sense of satisfaction through her.

For the next hour, they discussed any other details they might need to know in order to get their story straight. They'd stayed at the Windswept Resort in Cabo. The weather had been beautiful for their entire trip. Snorkeling at Chileno Bay had been amazing. Those were all the small details that they couldn't miss. They even had some photoshopped pictures on their phones to show people.

Ainsley knew she was smart, that she could handle all the particulars of the situation.

And Carter was brilliant.

However, the business executives they were meeting were also sharp. One hint of doubt, and these guys would see through them.

Then she and Carter would never find the information they were looking for.

That wasn't acceptable.

They had to get through this—for Jason's sake.

CHAPTER
SIX

AS AINSLEY DROVE, she glanced in the rearview mirror, searching for any signs of danger. She couldn't be too careful.

However, for the past hour, the same car had been behind them.

It could be a coincidence. She and Carter *were* on the highway, and a lot of people traveled this road.

The car wasn't directly behind them but stayed back a comfortable distance. The tinted windows, along with a glare, didn't allow Ainsley to see who was behind the wheel or how many people were in the vehicle.

She glanced back at the highway ahead of her, her thoughts still churning.

She needed to make some calls.

Needed to give Charlie an update on the situation.

Needed to see if Dante Bacardi was still in jail.

Her stomach tightened.

The cops would've told her if he'd been released, right? But he wasn't supposed to get out for ten more years. Parole wasn't even on the table.

Her temples pounded.

Nothing made sense right now.

Ainsley knew she needed to remain sharp in order to successfully pull this whole charade off.

But that rose messed with her mind.

What if Dante was somehow back? What if he was watching her?

What if he was driving the vehicle behind them?

The ache at her temples pulsed even stronger.

"Is everything okay?" Carter glanced at her.

Ainsley swallowed hard and tried to relax her shoulders. "Of course."

She'd have to be careful around him. He was smart. Maybe too smart for his own good. She didn't want to alarm him for no reason. As a woman in a predominately male career, she had to work extra hard to make those around her trust her abilities. That was simply a fact of life.

Her gaze skimmed to the rearview mirror again.

The car was still there.

As an exit approached, Ainsley spontaneously pulled off the highway.

"This isn't the way to Aspen." Carter's forehead wrinkled with confusion.

"I know. I need to get gas."

He narrowed his gaze as he glanced at the dash. "You have a half tank."

"You know how it is in these mountains. It's better to fill up when you can. My dad taught me that. It was one of his stipulations when I got my first car."

He gave her a look but said nothing.

As Ainsley pulled into the gas station, the car behind her didn't follow.

Her shoulders loosened slightly.

Maybe Dante wasn't out of prison and stalking her again.

But the mere possibility absolutely terrified her.

She might be a bodyguard and a former Texas Ranger but, when it came to Dante, he messed with her mind so much that her fears threatened to overpower her training.

She couldn't let that happen.

Too much was riding on this assignment.

Carter didn't know what was going through Ainsley's mind. Maybe it was better he didn't know. In the past, she'd consumed his thoughts until everything else disappeared.

He couldn't afford to let that happen now, no matter how tempting.

He glanced around the gas station as Ainsley finished filling up.

Carter had offered to pump gas for her, but she'd insisted on doing it herself. He remembered her stubbornness and had decided not to argue. Not this time, at least.

Instead, he took the opportunity to check his phone.

He hadn't made a secret of the fact he was going on this trip. However, he hadn't told his friends about his so-called marriage. He'd thought about doing so before he left, but he had decided against it.

It was one thing to lie to strangers or people he did business with—not that he practiced doing that or thought it was right. But it was an entirely different story to lie to people he cared about.

Most of his friends didn't know about Ainsley. Carter wasn't exactly the type who went on and on about his love life and heartbreak. Some things—like love and even business deals—were best kept private.

Before he could check his emails, his phone buzzed.

He glanced at the screen, and his lungs froze.

A text from an unknown number appeared.

You can't trust her. You'll regret it if you do.

He sucked in a breath. Who had sent this? Did someone know what he was planning?

Was this person talking about Ainsley?

They had to be. No one else made sense.

Carter glanced at Ainsley as she placed the gas nozzle back into the pump. The woman might look innocent. But was she keeping secrets?

He needed to call Charlie and have a long conversation. He liked this whole charade less and less all the time.

As he saw Ainsley studying something in the distance, Carter craned his neck. A dark sedan slowly pulled into the lot.

When Carter glanced at Ainsley again, he noticed her shoulders had stiffened.

That's when he knew something was wrong.

Who was inside that car?

Could it be the person who'd left the bomb that killed Maureen?

CHAPTER
SEVEN

AINSLEY WATCHED as a charcoal-gray sedan pulled to a stop near the curb only ten feet away from Ainsley and Carter.

Was that the same vehicle that had followed behind them on the highway? Had the driver taken another exit, then turned around and backtracked to get here?

Ainsley held her breath as she waited for whatever would happen next.

As the car door opened, she braced herself.

Started to reach for the gun she'd shoved into her waistband.

A man emerged . . .

Followed by a woman and two small children.

Ainsley released the air from her lungs and slipped her hand from her purse.

She'd gotten worked up for nothing.

Then she remembered the rose.

This *wasn't* nothing. She and Carter were meeting with the man who'd potentially killed her brother. An innocent bystander had been murdered in front of their eyes today. And a rose reminiscent of the greatest nightmare of her life had been left for her.

It was a lot for anyone to handle.

Composing herself, Ainsley climbed back into her SUV.

She felt Carter's gaze on her and knew the details of what had just happened hadn't slipped by him. The man was astute and could read her more than she liked to admit.

"Everything okay?" He studied her face.

Ainsley cranked the engine. "It's just fine. We better get going."

Carter didn't ask any more questions. Not now.

The bad feeling in Ainsley's gut continued to grow.

She'd been in a lot of sticky situations as a Texas Ranger, and she knew how to handle herself.

But the stakes of this assignment were personal.

Several minutes later, they turned off the highway and onto the smaller winding road leading to Aspen.

The snow became thicker as they climbed higher, and Ainsley gripped the wheel harder.

"Do you want me to drive?" Carter asked. "I'm used to being in the mountains."

She knew what he was getting at. The area where she'd grown up was mostly flat.

But there was no place to pull over here.

"I've got it," she muttered.

But no sooner had she said the words did she hear a pop.

Her SUV began swerving over the icy road, dangerously close to a guardrail.

———

Carter gripped the handle above him as the SUV slid across the road.

What had just happened?

Ainsley tensed, her knuckles white as she gripped the steering wheel.

As the guardrail appeared in front of them, he braced himself for an impact.

Braced himself to plunge off the cliff on the other side.

But, before that could happen, Ainsley jerked the wheel.

The SUV turned, scraping the guardrail. Squeals filled the air. The smell of burning rubber.

Then the vehicle straightened.

Coasted.

And Ainsley pulled to a stop on the other side of the road, near a rocky mountain slope. Smoke came from the hood, and the side of the SUV was definitely scraped.

But they hadn't gone off the cliff.

They both sat there a moment without saying anything.

Carter's heart pounded at a fast tempo against his chest.

Finally, he turned to Ainsley and asked, "Are you okay?"

Ainsley glanced at him, obviously shaken, but she nodded. "I think so. You?"

"All things considered, I'm fine. What happened?"

"That's what we need to figure out. But I think one of my tires popped."

"How is that possible?"

"I think someone may have set us up." She swallowed so hard that she rubbed her neck. "Let me check it out."

He grabbed her arm. "I'll look."

There were some things he could step back and let her do. But right now, Carter wanted to take care of this situation.

To his surprise, Ainsley didn't argue.

He climbed out, pulled his sweatshirt around his neck as the wind blew around him.

He hoped no other cars came around this bend. This road was not the one you wanted to be broken down on.

Circling to the front of the SUV, he saw the tire.

It was flatter than a pancake.

He knelt to examine it and saw the small slash there.

Ainsley was right.

Someone had done this on purpose.

———

What had seemed like a cut-and-dried assignment was turning into anything but.

The good news was that Carter had been able to reach Jack, who promised to send someone to pick them up.

In the meantime, they sat in the SUV and waited.

"Why try to take us out so early?" Carter asked.

Ainsley had thought about that also. "It's a war tactic."

"What do you mean?"

She shrugged. "Sometimes, you want to make your enemy feel weak. I don't think the person who did this wanted us to die. This person just wanted to scare us. To throw us off our game. That's probably why Maureen was killed also."

"Someone has a sick idea of what it means to play a game."

"Whoever is behind the bombing has gotten away with it for years. They don't want to be caught now. I'm guessing your father knew something incriminating, and that's why he was killed."

Carter didn't argue.

A few minutes of silence passed before he finally said, "For the record, I don't need a bodyguard."

Ainsley's eyebrows shot up at his words, which seemed to come out of nowhere.

Carter had known Charlie was sending someone. He just hadn't known it was Ainsley. Why all the hostility now?

His shock must be wearing off.

She locked her gaze with his. "For the record, I beg to differ."

Carter bristled. "Charlie said she was sending someone to watch my back."

"You don't think I can watch your back?"

"All I'm saying is that with our history—it's . . . complicated."

Ainsley started to retort, but instead she pressed her lips together.

She knew no man wanted a bodyguard—nonetheless a *female* bodyguard. Especially not a macho guy like Carter.

No, he wasn't former military or law enforcement. But he still gave off an air of toughness. He'd been an athlete and had played football in both high school and college, so he was strong.

But there was a difference between being strong and being trained for dangerous situations. Plus, everyone needed someone to watch their back in certain situations.

That could prove to be one of the difficult parts of this assignment.

Ainsley didn't trust Carter.

Perhaps Carter didn't trust Ainsley.

"I'm only going along with this because Charlie insisted it was smart not to come at this alone," Carter finally said in a sharp whisper. "She said a pretend relationship wouldn't raise any eyebrows. She didn't mention you—and I plan on talking to her about that."

Ainsley scowled. "Look, I don't like this any more than you do. She said the two of us made more sense. Besides, the one other full-time female agent at Vanishing Ranch is already married, so that would be a little weird. Since we know each other, we won't look like two strangers trying to mesh."

His eyes narrowed. "Instead, we might come

across as newlyweds who secretly despise each other."

"*You* despise *me*?" Ainsley hadn't meant to say the words aloud, but they'd slipped out.

What had she ever done to Carter to make *him* have hard feelings?

Carter was the one Ainsley had found in the arms of another woman less than an hour after they'd shared their first kiss!

She turned toward him. "Look, we just have to get through the weekend. This isn't exactly ideal for me either, you know."

"Ainsley . . ." Carter opened his mouth as if he wanted to say something.

The last thing she wanted was to hear an apology or an excuse.

What happened sixteen years ago was over and done with. Carter didn't need to dredge up that history. Plus, the thought of them talking about their past somehow made her feel weak.

Ainsley didn't like feeling weak.

"I could have said no when Charlie contacted me," Carter finally said with a dismissive shrug. "Once I heard her theory, I could have done this on my own."

"Only if you wanted to put your life on the line."

He shifted, his hands going to his hips. "You aren't giving me enough credit."

"No, *you're* not giving *me* enough credit."

Before they could argue anymore, their ride pulled up.

They were going to have to save the rest of this conversation until later.

CHAPTER EIGHT

THIRTY MINUTES LATER, Carter and Ainsley arrived at The Everly resort.

Back when Carter had been younger, this area had been one of his favorites. He'd felt like a real jetsetter when he'd come to Aspen.

Everything about the area *was* nice. He couldn't deny that.

But time had taught him that wealth wasn't the end-all. That's why, now that Carter had sold his business, he'd devoted his free time to finishing the encryption program his father had been working on.

He had a feeling that very encryption program was what had gotten his father killed. Whatever information was hiding behind those firewalls was valuable—and therefore dangerous.

Carter needed answers, and this weekend was his best chance to find them.

As their ride pulled in front of the lodge, two valets approached.

A few minutes later, their bags were on their way up to the room, and Ainsley and Carter stood beside each other near the entrance as a frigid wind whipped around them.

This was it.

The make-or-break moment.

So far, they hadn't gotten off to a good start.

Ainsley glanced up at him. "Are you ready for this?"

Her eyes looked just as crystal blue and intriguing as ever.

This whole charade would be much harder than Carter had ever imagined.

Especially with Ainsley here.

Especially considering the fact that Maureen had just died.

Especially since he'd gotten that text.

But mostly because his father had been killed over whatever secret agenda was at play. The people behind this—most likely Jack and his cronies—would stop at nothing to get what they wanted.

Carter turned to Ainsley. "I'm ready. You?"

She nodded and held out her arm. Carter placed

his hand in hers, relishing the soft, supple feel of her skin.

Relishing?

That was the last thing he should be doing.

He needed to find Jack.

They were supposed to have dinner together this evening.

The sooner he and Ainsley could find the answers they sought, the sooner this whole thing would be over.

And Carter would finally have justice for his father's death.

But first, they had to put on the show of their lives.

As he glanced up, he saw a security camera above them. A red dot flashed on it, and the lens was aimed right at Carter and Ainsley.

He almost felt like someone was already watching their every move.

Maybe that's because they were.

———

"If it isn't Carter Winslow!"

Carter and Ainsley both turned toward the voice.

Carter sucked in a breath when he saw the man standing in the entryway.

The fifty-something man had olive skin and dark hair that he kept at chin length. He swept it back from his face in a way that made him seem both affluent and trendy. His body was trim—no doubt from a lot of time with a personal trainer—and he had a movie star, unnaturally perfect smile.

Jack Earl.

The man they needed to keep an eye on.

The man who could be responsible for hundreds of deaths.

Carter switched into professional mode and put his argument with Ainsley behind him as he turned toward Jack and extended his hand.

It was time to tap into his acting skills. He'd perfected them through the years as he'd learned the art of succeeding in business. He hated the fact that this came with the territory, but it did.

"Jack, my man . . . good to see you."

It had been several months since the two of them had seen each other. But they both ran in the same circles—Jack's more powerful and affluent than Carter's, however.

Still, it was nearly impossible for them to avoid each other since they worked in the same field.

"Heard you had some car trouble," Jack said. "I'm sorry to hear that. I sent another crew to tow your car here."

"I appreciate it." But, at the same time, Carter realized this meant he and Ainsley were stuck here with no easily accessible mode of transportation.

He didn't like that.

Especially since this resort was so secluded with only one mountain road leading here.

"I've probably told you this before, but you are the spitting image of your dad." Jack shook his head as he looked Carter up and down.

Carter raised his hands. "It's not the first time I've heard that. I'd like to think I'm a little more handsome, however." He grinned.

Jack smiled and turned to Ainsley. "Who is this lovely woman beside you?"

Carter slipped his arm around Ainsley's shoulders. "Jack, I'd like to introduce you to Ainsley . . . my wife."

Jack's eyebrows shot up. "Your wife? I hadn't heard. I thought I might get an invitation to the wedding whenever you took the plunge."

"It was all rather spontaneous, wasn't it, snookums?" Carter pulled Ainsley close and grinned at her.

"It sure was, boo bear. But when you know you know, right?"

Jack clapped his hands in front of him and grinned. "Well, I can't wait to hear that story. You can tell me tonight at dinner. I want to meet with you, but not to talk business or work or anything else that's not fun—just to have a good time. Are you two okay with that?"

"That sounds great," Carter told Jack. "Name the time and place."

"I'll have my assistant text it to you." He grinned again. "I can't wait to get to know you both more and introduce you to the rest of the team. But for tonight, it'll just be me and Haley—my other half."

"Sounds great."

Carter kept a smile plastered on his face as Jack moved away from them and stepped outside.

As soon as the man was out of sight, he released his breath.

They'd gotten through the initial meeting.

But this was only the beginning.

Things would get much more complicated from here.

AINSLEY'S THOUGHTS continued to race after meeting Jack.

Having dinner with him tonight would be perfect.

Jack said he didn't want to talk about business, but maybe they'd learn something that might help them find answers. However, Ainsley would have to be very casual if she brought up any touchy subjects.

The hardest part would be selling the fact that she and Carter were supposed to be newlyweds. It seemed the longer the two of them were around each other, the more the tension between them grew. Maybe that was because Carter's shock was slowly wearing off.

She knew there were a lot of unspoken conversations that should probably take place. But she had no desire to delve into the past, especially not her past with Carter.

Speaking of Carter . . .

She turned toward him as they stood in the lobby. "We should get to our room."

"Yes, we should." He took her hand and led her toward the front desk.

Ainsley shouldn't have fireworks going off in her head at the feel of his fingers tangled around hers. But she did. She'd *always* felt that way around Carter. She supposed some things never changed.

But you know what else made her feel tingles? Electricity.

And electricity could kill her.

She needed to remember that.

After getting their key cards, they took the elevator to the fourth floor and found their room. As soon as they walked in, Ainsley motioned for Carter to stay by the door.

Then she withdrew her gun and searched the suite to make sure it was safe.

"Is this really necessary?" Carter frowned as he lingered by the door.

"Only if you want to live," she said dryly.

Carter let out an airy chuckle. "I do like your directness. Nothing scares you, does it?"

There were many things that scared her. But few things that people knew about.

Love was at the top of that list.

And Carter was the reason why.

Ainsley *definitely* didn't want him to know that.

After she deemed the room safe—and after she checked it for bugs and cameras—she placed her gun back in her purse and stepped toward Carter. "It's all clear. How much time do we have before we meet Jack?"

He glanced at his phone and saw the text from Jack's assistant. "An hour."

Her phone buzzed, and she saw it was a text from Charlie.

Just did a little more research into Jack's executive assistant, a man named Eric Lemur. His family has ties with a terrorist group in the Middle East. Keep an eye on him.

Ainsley swallowed hard. She'd known that probably more than one person was involved in this. Had known that Jack was probably involved—but perhaps not the ringleader.

Suddenly, this whole situation was feeling an awful lot like a trap.

After Ainsley finished getting ready and Carter stepped into the bathroom, she pulled out her phone.

She needed to talk to Charlie—both about the text and to give her an update on the earlier events that had transpired.

Charlie answered on the first ring. "Hey, Ainsley. What's going on?"

"You didn't tell Carter I was the one he'd be working with?" She didn't bother with formalities.

"I'm sorry about that, but I thought he might refuse. You were the most natural choice. I knew the two of you would work things out."

Ainsley scowled and paced toward the window. "A heads-up would have been nice."

"I also knew you were a professional who could handle it. Are you handling it?"

"I suppose." Ainsley stood near the window staring outside. "But there have been some developments."

She filled her in on Maureen, the rose, and the slashed tire.

"Wait a minute . . . you had a man stalking you, but he's supposedly in prison now . . . and his trademark was leaving a yellow rose for you?" Charlie sounded confused.

Ainsley rubbed her neck as she felt her muscles stiffen. "I would've told you, but the whole stalking situation didn't seem significant when you hired me. I mean, Dante is supposed to be in prison, and I think I'd know if he was out. Someone would've told me."

"I don't like the sound of this." Charlie's voice tightened with protectiveness.

Ainsley continued to stare out the window at the snow-covered peaks in the distance. "Me either. Believe me."

"You still think you can handle this job?"

Ainsley's breath caught. This was it—her chance to get out of this assignment. All she had to do was tell Charlie she was in over her head, and Charlie would send someone else.

But she knew it was too late for that.

Jack had already seen her face. Besides, Ainsley wasn't a quitter. Her dad had impressed that trait upon her.

Ainsley raised her chin. "I'll be fine."

Charlie remained quiet before finally asking, "How are you and Carter getting along?"

Ainsley remembered their tense conversations and frowned. "Just fine. Easy peasy lemon squeezy."

Easy peasy lemon squeezy? Ainsley rolled her eyes. *Come on, Ainsley. You can do better than that.*

"Just fine?"

"That's right." Ainsley needed to believe that, with a little effort and some mind tricks, she could get through this.

"I'm going to send Hayes to help."

"Hayes?" Ainsley straightened with confusion. "Why are you sending Hayes?"

Hayes Barlow was another operative at Vanishing Ranch.

"I'll send him as a guest to the resort. No one will know the two of you are connected. But I want someone else on hand in case things turn ugly."

Ainsley glanced back at the bathroom door, still hearing the sound of the shower running. "Okay then. That sounds like a good idea."

"And, Ainsley?"

Ainsley gripped the phone harder. "Yes?"

"Please, be careful."

Was Charlie talking about Ainsley's heart or her physical safety during this assignment?

She swallowed hard. It didn't matter. She had the same answer for both.

Charlie's phone beeped as if she had another call coming in, and Ainsley knew they needed to wrap this up.

"Don't worry—I plan on being very guarded."

CARTER LEFT the water on in the shower in order to obscure the conversation he was about to have.

He dialed Charlie Soldier's number. He didn't think she would answer, but she finally did on the fourth ring.

"Carter . . ." Her voice trailed, almost as if she'd been expecting him.

"You didn't mention that Ainsley Tatum would be working with me." There was no need to beat around the bush.

"You would have said no."

"Of course, I would have!" Carter realized he'd raised his voice and drew in a deep breath. "You should have mentioned it."

"I had to make a call on that. I knew the two of you could work things out."

"I don't know . . ." He remembered their fiery conversations.

"Ainsley is a good operative," Charlie said. "And she's personally invested in this assignment. I trust that the two of you are strong enough to overcome your differences."

Carter thought about that text he'd gotten. *You can't trust her. You'll regret it if you do.*

He considered telling Charlie about it.

But he knew what Charlie would say. She'd claim Ainsley was trustworthy.

That's what Carter wanted to believe. But he wasn't sure he could.

"You got this?" Charlie asked.

Carter stared in the steamed mirror at his barely visible form and frowned. "I guess so."

"That's the spirit."

He frowned again before putting his phone away and drawing in a deep breath as he composed himself.

A moment later, he shut off the water and opened the bathroom door.

Across the room, he spotted Ainsley as she double-checked her makeup in a mirror.

She really had cleaned up nicely—she always had.

Back when he'd known her, she favored dusty

jeans, rock and roll T-shirts, and cowboy boots.

Right now, she wore black pants, an ivory turtle-neck, and ankle boots.

She still looked like a knockout.

Carter had known from the very first time he'd seen Ainsley that something was different about her. Something fascinating. Something that brought out his curiosity like no other woman ever had.

He'd wanted to peel back her layers. Learn every-thing he could about her: What made her tick. What she liked. What she didn't like. The events that made her into the person she was.

But he'd missed out on that chance, and he'd regretted it ever since.

"Are you ready to go, cowboy?" Ainsley stared up at him with that carefree sound to her voice.

He raised an eyebrow. "Cowboy? I think you and I both know, of all things, I'm *not* a cowboy."

He'd been a city slicker through and through, born and raised in New York.

A small, almost sad grin played across Ainsley's lips. "True. But way back when, I hoped maybe you could be."

His gaze caught hers. "Did you?"

She shrugged nonchalantly, any hint of her earlier nostalgia quickly disappearing, replaced with what looked like regret. "I mean, once I taught you how to ride a horse, you were pretty good at it."

"I had a good teacher."

Carter couldn't be sure, but he thought her cheeks heated. The feelings and tension between them had exploded during the hours they'd spent together on horseback. Certainly, Ainsley remembered that also.

They'd practically been inseparable—especially when Jason had gotten an unexpected internship that kept him away from the ranch.

She cleared her throat and nodded toward the door. "We should go."

"Yes, we should." The conversation had been a nice distraction from the impending conversations at dinner. Plus, their chat had almost been pleasant.

That was a welcome change.

Carter didn't get nervous very often. But he knew how much was riding on this weekend. He had to locate the information he'd come here to find.

He opened the door to leave for dinner.

But something stopped him from stepping out.

A yellow rose lay on the carpet at his feet.

———

Ainsley froze—but only for a moment before snapping into action.

"Get back," she ordered Carter.

She reached into her purse and withdrew her gun.

Then she stepped from the room and glanced down the hallway.

But she saw no one.

If someone here knew about her past, that could put this whole investigation in jeopardy.

She couldn't let that happen.

"Ainsley?" Carter's voice sounded strained.

She placed the gun back into her purse before picking up the rose. "Whoever left this is gone."

"I don't like this." His voice sounded deep and almost protective.

Ainsley swallowed hard.

No, she was imagining that protectiveness. Carter had no reason to feel the need to keep her safe. None of what she'd felt between the two of them was real —not on his part, at least.

He stepped closer and stared down at her. "What do you want to do?"

She set the rose on a table near the door and turned back to him. "We can't afford to be late. We're going to this meeting."

Concern flooded his gaze. "But—"

"I'll worry about that rose later."

Questions flashed in his eyes, questions she

couldn't answer right now.

Instead, she led him into the hall.

Then she took his arm. "We're going to have to concentrate if we're going to pull this off."

Carter studied her another moment. "I suppose we are. But I'm worried about—"

"There's no time to deal with anything else right now. We need to get going. If we're late, that won't make a good impression."

Ainsley knew he couldn't argue with that statement, even if he wanted to. Which no doubt he did.

She prayed he couldn't feel the tremor that raked through her as her emotions churned inside her.

CARTER DIDN'T LIKE any of this.

Coming here to The Everly was a bad idea.

Being here with Ainsley was a *terrible* idea.

It wasn't too late to back out.

But he wasn't sure if he'd ever get this opportunity with Jack Earl again.

Jack had brought Carter here to wine and dine him, as the saying went.

He was doing everything in his power to get Carter to work for him on a special project. Agreeing to it would give him a good opportunity to find some answers.

Somewhere, there was a paper trail—or a digital one—that would lead to the truth.

Someone didn't simply bomb a hotel without

leaving some kind of evidence. The planning and the people involved would have been extensive.

The FBI had insisted terrorists were behind it.

And—not to defend terrorists—but in this case, they'd been set up. Military operations had ensued.

But it was all part of a bigger plan.

He was sure of it.

As the elevator dinged, Carter and Ainsley stepped off. A few turns later, Carter spotted one of the resort's many restaurants.

Classical music played overhead as glasses clinked and silverware pinged against porcelain plates. The scent of steak and seafood filled the air. In the background, an entire wall of windows displayed the beautiful Rocky Mountains and White River National Forest in all its glory.

If only he were here to enjoy himself.

"Here goes nothing," Ainsley muttered.

As they stepped toward the hostess stand, Carter searched the crowds.

His gaze stopped on Jack.

He stood inside near the restaurant's patio, whispering to a man Carter didn't recognize.

Whatever they were talking about, their conversation appeared intense.

"That's Eric Lemur," Ainsley explained.

She'd already told him about the man's potential

ties with terrorists. The executive assistant wasn't a young buck right out of college either. He was in his forties—old enough that he could somehow have been involved with that bombing.

"I'd love to be a fly on the wall right now," Carter muttered.

"You and me both."

"Good evening." The sound of the hostess's voice snapped them from their conversation. "Do you have a reservation?"

"We do." Carter rattled off his name.

The perky hostess smiled as she grabbed two menus. "Welcome, Mr. and Mrs. Winslow."

Carter swallowed, feeling an unwelcome shot of delight at hearing "Mr. and Mrs. Winslow." It had a nice ring to it.

But he reminded himself again that he wasn't sure if he could trust Ainsley.

He kept his face composed as he said, "That's correct. Mr. and Mrs. Winslow. We're meeting Jack Earl."

The hostess beamed. "Mr. Earl has done wonderful things with this place ever since he took over."

"Took over?" Carter twisted his neck in confusion.

The woman tilted her head in surprise. "You

didn't know? He doesn't like to brag. But, yes, he bought this resort last year and has been revitalizing it, bringing it back to the grandeur it once held."

If Jack owned this place . . . that meant he would have access to all the staff and even security camera footage.

That could make things more complicated.

Carter exchanged a look with Ainsley as the hostess led them to their seats.

Ainsley's expression made it clear that her thoughts mirrored his.

———

Ainsley plastered on a smile as she approached the table with their hostess.

Jack owned this place? Why hadn't that factoid popped up when she and Charlie had been doing their research?

Jack had probably bought the resort under the name of one of his corporations. But that didn't make her feel any better.

She was in enemy territory right now.

As they reached the table, Jack joined them, and Ainsley tried to loosen her muscles.

"Carter. Ainsley. I'm so glad you could both make

it." He extended his hand toward the stunning woman already seated. "This is Haley."

They all exchanged hellos.

Ainsley noted that Haley seemed cool and aloof. Her smile didn't reach her eyes. But she was definitely a woman a guy like Jack Earl would want to have on his arm.

With Carter's gentlemanly assistance, Ainsley tucked herself into the chair at the table and he sat across from her. They had several minutes of small talk, mostly about the resort.

As the waiter filled their goblets with water, Ainsley glanced at the menu.

For a moment, she felt out of place. She wasn't rich and fancy. Never had been. Never wanted to be.

She was a country girl who'd grown up on rodeos, horses, and barbecue.

This world wasn't hers. There was no way she could afford eating at a place like this—not during her childhood or even now. None of her jobs ever paid enough for such a lifestyle.

She usually didn't let that fact get the best of her. But right now, she was all too aware of her lower socioeconomic status.

She couldn't let those thoughts take root or she would blow her cover.

"Excuse me . . ." someone said beside her.

Ainsley looked over and saw a sixty-something man and woman staring at her.

She instantly bristled. "Yes?"

"Aren't you that woman who won the bull riding championship several years ago?"

Ainsley willed her cheeks not to flush. "You must have me mistaken for someone else."

"You look just like her," the man continued. "She was *amazing*. No other women ever even attempted to try their skills bull riding. But she did. I can't remember her name. But she was a real inspiration. Even got my daughter interested in the rodeo."

Ainsley forced a smile. "This woman does sound inspiring. I'll have to look her up."

The man nodded and frowned. "You do that. I'm sorry to interrupt your dinner."

Ainsley told him it was okay.

But she had bigger fears than an interrupted dinner.

She hoped her cover hadn't just been blown.

CHAPTER
TWELVE

AINSLEY SQUARED HER SHOULDERS, praying as she glanced back at Jack that he didn't seem either curious or suspicious.

But his expression remained the same—plastered with a smile and barely concealed impatience.

She glanced back at the menu, not wanting to give that conversation any more unnecessary attention. But every once in a while, she glanced over Jack's shoulder and surveyed everyone around them.

So far, she hadn't seen anyone suspicious. Was the person who left the rose watching them now? Did Jack have people working for him, acting as a second set of eyes and ears?

There were a lot of uncertainties right now—far more than she was comfortable with.

After the waitress took their orders, the questions began.

"So . . . I'm anxious to hear about this quick courtship and marriage that you mentioned." Jack looked over at Haley and squeezed her hand. "I know someone else who wouldn't mind a quick courtship and marriage, but I'm not sure I'm in for it. That doesn't mean I don't love you, dear."

That barely there smile whispered across Haley's face, again not reaching her eyes.

Ainsley turned to Carter. "Do you want to tell him, or do you want me to?"

"Well, for starters, isn't it obvious why I snatched her up while I could?" Carter's eyes sparkled as his gaze lingered on her.

"Your wife is quite beautiful," Jack said. "No one can deny that."

"From the moment I saw Ainsley, I knew I wanted to get to know her better. I was actually down in Mexico on a working vacation. I was at the beach, sitting in a lounge chair and catching up on some correspondence. When I saw her walk past, my concentration was shot."

Jack grinned as if he liked where the story was going. "Continue."

Ainsley took over.

"He wasn't shy. He walked right up to me and

asked if I'd like to have dinner with him that night." She paused for dramatic effect. "I told him no."

Jack's eyebrows shot up.

"It was a little bit of a blow to my ego," Carter said. "But I'm not one to be deterred."

"Just one more thing to like about you." Jack nodded with certainty. "Those traits go far in business."

"I like to think so too," Carter said. "So when I ran into Ainsley later in the resort lobby, I asked her on a date again. She said if I beat her at cornhole, she'd accept."

"He agreed, and he did beat me—but only because I let him." Ainsley winked playfully at Carter. "We spent the rest of our vacation together. I knew after the third day that I'd be a fool to let him walk away."

"And I knew that the first time I saw her. So I'm truly the winner here." Carter winked at her in return.

Ainsley let out a little giggle. "We knew it was crazy, and I'm not usually the spontaneous type. But a week later, we decided to elope. Why not, especially since we both knew that's what we wanted? So we got married, spent our last week of vacation together in Mexico, and then came back to the States. Now, here we are on an extended honeymoon."

"What a story." Jack shook his head, appearing fascinated. "I've always heard about these insta-love types of moments, but I don't meet very many people who actually experience it. I wish you both the best of luck with this new marriage. You seem well-suited for each other."

"I like to think so." Ainsley reached across the table and squeezed Carter's hand.

As Ainsley said the words, she realized that much of her story would've been true—sixteen years ago. Not the location or the fine details.

But from the moment she and Carter had met, they'd hit it off. She'd had a mad crush on her brother's best friend. The boy who liked to tug her hair. Who liked to pick her up and turn her in circles until she was dizzy.

Over the summer, their interactions had grown into something much more than that.

Until Ainsley realized it was all a lie.

She fought a frown.

Just like this was all a lie.

A lie that her life depended on.

———

Reliving those memories—however fake they had been—had felt a little too real for Carter. A little too close to the truth.

He tried not to let his mind reel back in time.

But it was hard, considering Ainsley was sitting beside him.

The rest of the conversation with Jack had been casual—much of it about the mountains here in Aspen and the resort. Their food had come, and they'd eaten.

Since Jack owned the place, the waitress didn't bother to bring a check. Instead, Jack had presented her with a substantial tip for what he called her "sublime" service.

Altogether, the dinner had been pleasant. Haley had been quiet and looked rather bored. Carter wasn't surprised. Jack hadn't paid any attention to her.

Ainsley, however, was doing a good job putting on the show of her life.

But Carter had to admit that he was worried about her.

The rose had left him feeling disturbed, to say the least.

Someone knew Ainsley was here. Could one of Jack's men be onto them? Could they have heard about Dante and decided to taunt her with the roses?

He didn't know.

Carter knew Ainsley was tough. She'd proven that before.

But if these guys were as deadly as he thought, then she might be in over her head. They were secluded out here. Without many resources. Not on neutral territory.

"Carter, I'd love to chat with you one-on-one. Why don't you and I take a little walk around the resort while the ladies grab something hot to drink over at the coffeeshop?"

Carter glanced at Ainsley, not liking the sound of that idea but trying not to show it. If he protested, it could look suspicious.

"Are you sure the ladies can't come?" Carter tried to sound casual. "They make us look a lot better."

Jack laughed as if he agreed with that sentiment. "Yes, they do. But there's a time where men should talk as men, and women should talk as women. This is one of them. I know the two of you are newlyweds, but I promise some time apart won't hurt you. I should know. I've been married four times."

Jack released a loud chuckle.

But Carter still felt uneasy.

Did Jack want to separate them for a reason? Did he know who Ainsley really was?

Carter wouldn't put anything past Jack.

He glanced at Ainsley and tried to read her expression. But her thoughts were well hidden.

"Some coffee with Haley sounds wonderful," Ainsley finally said. "As was dinner. Everything was delicious, and the company marvelous. Thank you for inviting me and letting me come along on this little business trip."

Her poise in this situation gave Carter a moment of pause. He wondered what his life would be like right now if things had turned out differently between them.

Having Ainsley at his side would have changed everything. Though their lifestyles had been worlds apart, he felt confident they could have made things work.

He also reminded himself not to trust her too much. It wouldn't be smart. Not considering the stakes here.

"It's my pleasure." Jack turned back to Carter. "Now you and me . . . let's go talk."

But just as they stood, someone in the lobby behind them yelled.

They turned and saw a man racing through the building.

He raised a gun in the air—and he was headed right toward them.

CHAPTER
THIRTEEN

AINSLEY FORCED herself not to reach for her gun.

Not yet.

But who was that man?

She watched as he raced toward them.

Two security guards followed.

Before they reached the restaurant, they tackled the man.

His gun skittered across the floor.

And everyone around them seemed to let out a collective sigh of relief.

"You're going to pay!" the man shouted as he glanced at Jack.

The security guards handcuffed him and jerked him to his feet.

"I promise you, you'll pay!" the man yelled over his shoulder as the guards led him away.

Ainsley glanced at Jack who shrugged. "I know that seems dramatic, but people do crazy things. I can't count the number of threats I get every day."

"You seem so . . . unbothered by this," Ainsley muttered.

He shrugged again. "I have top-notch security."

"What did that guy mean?" Carter asked. "That you'll pay?"

"People have all kinds of crazy conspiracy theories. Or if something bad happened on social media, they blame me. There could be any number of reasons. None of them are important. I promise you."

Ainsley wasn't so sure about that.

"Carter . . . you and I . . . let's talk."

Jack was not easily deterred, was he?

Ainsley glanced at Carter. She didn't want to leave him. But she knew at this point that protesting would only raise suspicions. Ainsley didn't think Jack would pull any stunts on their first night here.

The man was trying to woo Carter, not kill him.

Besides, maybe she could get some information from Haley.

When she glanced at the stoic woman, she doubted it.

As the two of them walked to a coffeeshop in the distance, Ainsley's phone buzzed.

It was a text message from Charlie.

Everett Maurice died in a mysterious boating accident in Florida two days ago.

Ainsley tried not to show any emotion on her face.

But she knew exactly why the man had died.

Because of Jack Earl.

This place was suddenly feeling smaller and smaller, almost like the walls were closing in.

———

As Ainsley sipped on some hot chocolate by the fireplace, she tried to stop thinking about Everett. But his death dominated her thoughts.

This was all connected. She knew it was.

But she'd have time to dwell on that later.

Instead, she turned to Haley, keeping her expression even.

Ainsley had a feeling the woman was smarter than she let on. Behind that bored gaze, there was a calculating mind. No doubt, she had seen and heard things. She'd been privy to Jack's comings and goings.

But would she open up?

Ainsley cleared her throat. "So, how long have you and Jack been together?"

"Three months," Haley answered, looking uninterested.

"How did the two of you meet?"

"Through mutual friends."

"He seems like quite a guy," Ainsley said. "It must be fun to go along on all his adventures."

"I suppose."

What exactly could Ainsley ask this woman that might get her talking? She was running out of ideas. If there was one thing Ainsley hated it was awkward conversations.

There had to be *something* that could spike Haley's interest.

"So . . . do you go with him on a lot of business trips?"

Haley offered a half shrug. "My fair share. But they're pretty boring. Business leaders and politicians might be interesting to others, but not to me."

"Politicians?" Maybe this conversation *would* lead somewhere.

Haley shrugged again. "Those people are always

wanting something from Jack. Sometimes I feel a little sorry for him."

"I can imagine." Ainsley leaned back, trying to look casual. "Who has he met with? I'm intrigued."

"Believe me, I'll bore you—and myself—if I tell you. It's better if you tune all that out and look pretty. That's what men really want anyway."

Ainsley didn't like the sound of that. She was the type who believed she could do whatever she set her mind to. She definitely wasn't going to let her gender hold her back from opportunities. In fact, that very mindset drove her crazy.

As a woman, she was not a second-class citizen.

She also wasn't a decoration.

She wanted to say as much but, before she could, a figure in the distance caught her eye.

A man with dark hair and a ruddy complexion.

A man who almost looked like . . . Dante.

CARTER TRIED to concentrate on his conversation with Jack, but it was proving to be difficult. Mostly, the man wanted to talk about the resort. They stood near the windows, staring at the ski slopes in the distance.

He'd hoped to keep an eye on Ainsley as he and Jack talked.

He tried not to stare when he saw her rise and head down the hallway in the distance.

Where was she going?

He knew she was supposed to be protecting him.

And he wasn't so macho that the thought rattled him. Not totally, at least.

But he still preferred to be the protector.

It was how he'd been raised.

As Jack began another long speech about the resort, Carter followed Ainsley's figure with his gaze.

She strode toward something in the distance—and she moved quickly as if she were on a mission.

Had she seen someone?

Maybe the man who'd left those yellow roses?

Carter's muscles went rigid at the thought of it.

"Everything okay?" Jack squinted as he studied Carter's face.

He snapped his attention back to Jack. "It's more than okay. But I need to run to the restroom. Could you excuse me a moment?"

"Of course."

Carter meandered from the area, trying not to look too anxious or hurried. When he reached the restroom, he looked back and saw that Jack had turned away and already had his phone to his ear.

Carter quickly redirected his steps toward the hallway he'd seen Ainsley walk down.

But she wasn't there.

Where had she gone?

He glanced around the large lobby and didn't see her anywhere.

What if that stalker guy had grabbed her?

Urgency raced through his blood like wildfire.

Carter needed to find her.

There was no time to waste.

He stepped farther into the hallway, turned a corner, and spotted Ainsley.

Staying close to the wall, he tried not to make a scene. Ainsley probably wouldn't appreciate the fact he was following her.

But he couldn't seem to stop himself. Not when so much was at stake.

As he glanced up, he saw a man hiding behind a thick wooden post in the distance.

Carter bristled.

He had to warn Ainsley.

———

Ainsley lost sight of the man.

She wasn't sure where he'd gone. Wasn't sure if he was Dante. Wasn't sure about anything.

Her lungs felt tight at the thought of him. At the memories of her hands and feet being tied up. Of being at his mercy in a root cellar where she'd been certain no one would ever find her.

She'd gone to therapy after the ordeal. But panic threatened to overtake her now.

She paused near the wall but didn't see anyone.

Time was ticking away.

She frowned as she realized she needed to get

back to Haley. She couldn't afford to raise the woman's suspicions.

Ainsley drew in a deep breath to compose herself. Then she started back toward the fireplace.

As she rounded the corner, a man stepped in front of her.

And she braced herself for a fight.

AINSLEY'S HANDS FISTED.

Then Carter's face appeared.

The air left her lungs in a whoosh. She glanced around, checking to see if anyone was watching before whispering, "What are you doing here?"

He pulled her into an alcove, still staring at something in the distance. "I thought you might be in trouble."

"Me? In trouble?" Did Ainsley need to remind him that *she* was the one who was supposed to be watching *him*?

Carter nodded at someone lingering behind a wooden pillar near the corner.

Her heart rate quickened.

Then the fit, dark-haired man stepped into full view.

Hayes. Hayes was here, she realized.

He wasn't the man she'd seen earlier.

She wasn't sure where he'd gone or who he was.

But she'd need to remain on guard.

She quickly introduced the two men, putting aside her irritation with Carter.

"I left the ranch as soon as I heard." Hayes's gaze flickered behind them as he quickly surveyed the area. "The roads are getting bad as more snow moves in. Anyway, I just pulled up and saw you were here, so I decided to keep an eye out."

"Glad you made it, but we need to get back before Jack or any of his men see us talking." Ainsley looked around before facing Hayes again. "The two of us will be in touch later. But it's best if no one knows we're connected."

He offered a quick salute. "Couldn't agree more. You know how to reach me if you need me. In the meantime, I'll be blending in. If anyone asks, I own a meal delivery startup, and I'm going through a divorce and trying to recover."

A certain wistfulness entered his voice at the words.

Was there some truth to them?

Ainsley wasn't sure. She and Hayes were both new at Vanishing Ranch, and she didn't know his story yet.

But she was glad he was here.

They could use some backup.

That was becoming abundantly clear.

———

Ainsley looped her arm through Carter's so they could talk closely without being heard as they walked away from Hayes. Even though her voice and body language might sound and look pleasant, she felt anything but.

"I had the situation handled," she whispered.

"After these roses you've been getting, I'm not sure about that."

She swallowed hard, wanting to refute the statement. But she couldn't.

Still, this trip wasn't about her. Carter's safety was her main concern.

She could deal with those roses *and* do her job.

"I just need you to concentrate on Jack," she muttered instead. "Any progress?"

Carter shook his head. "Not yet. You?"

"Haley's like the ice queen."

A smile tugged at Carter's lips. "I had that impression also. But don't let her fool you. She graduated from Harvard."

Harvard? Maybe Haley was someone Ainsley needed to keep her eyes on after all. Haley and Eric.

Were they in this with Jack? Or did they have their own agendas?

As Ainsley and Carter paused near the center of the lobby, Carter leaned toward her and gave her a quick kiss on the cheek.

Ainsley's breath caught.

Why had he done that?

And why did her body have to react with a burst of warmth?

Her mind reeled back in time. Reeled back to the moment where she'd won the championship at the rodeo. Excitement had buzzed through the air.

She'd found Carter, who'd been there watching her. He would leave to head back to college the next day. He'd taken her hand and led her behind one of the buildings.

Then, after an entire summer of flirting and teasing, they'd shared a kiss.

Shared a kiss that had nearly blown her socks off.

She'd never been on cloud nine like that before.

She had to leave him in order to do some photos.

But when she found him again, he'd been kissing another woman.

Lillian.

His girlfriend, she'd found out later.

"Jack is watching," Carter's voice pulled her from her thoughts. "I need to tell him I ran into you and that's why I took so long."

"Makes sense." Ainsley forced a grin as she looked up at him.

Carter was right. They needed to look like two newlyweds who were madly in love.

Tonight, they needed to make a good impression.

Hopefully, tomorrow they'd find the information they needed.

A mental timer ticked down the minutes they had left to successfully complete this assignment.

Failure would mean more innocent people died and more evil men got away with their deeds.

CHAPTER
SIXTEEN

CARTER'S MEETING with Jack had led nowhere. Carter now knew what golf courses the man liked, why Jack felt Mercedes was a superior vehicle, and the list of every professional sports team worth rooting for.

In essence, Carter had been shown what his life could be like if he joined Jack's company. He'd have access to unfiltered wealth, lavish vacations, an over-sized home—or two or three—and any woman he wanted.

Yes, any woman. That was the implication Jack had given.

When a man like Jack was on a power trip, he didn't like boundaries of any sort—including when it came to romantic commitments.

This was the art of the business deal. Show people

what they wanted—or, maybe he should say, what they didn't even know they wanted.

Then later, after they'd been hooked and were salivating for those rewards, share the cost while downplaying what that price truly meant.

Things like losing your soul, integrity, self-worth.

Carter frowned.

It was too early in this game to make any plays tonight.

But tomorrow . . .

When there was a pause in the conversation, Carter glanced at his watch. "Listen, I should probably get back to Ainsley. I told her I wouldn't be too long."

Jack chuckled. "Newlyweds . . . I get it. We'll meet again in the morning. Sound good? I'll have my assistant send you a schedule."

Two of Jack's business partners would have arrived by then, and negotiations would begin. Hopefully, they'd be able to truly get down to business—and Carter could find out what he needed to know.

"Sounds good." Carter extended his hand. "It's great to be here."

"It's great to have you here."

As Carter walked by the fireplace, he noted that Ainsley and Haley were already gone.

Had they headed back to their rooms?

He hoped that was the case, but concern rushed through him. There was too much going on for him to feel comfortable.

As he started toward the elevator, he glanced around, looking for any signs of trouble. At least, Hayes would be here. That made Carter feel a little better.

Before he reached the elevator, his phone buzzed.

He paused and took the device from his pocket.

It was a message—from the same number as the one he'd gotten earlier.

He hesitated a moment before clicking on it.

The stark words staring back at him put him on edge.

Check her purse.

He glanced around. Who had sent this?

Was that person watching him right now?

The one thing Carter knew for certain was that this person had the power to ruin his whole plan.

And to potentially hurt him. To hurt Ainsley.

His gut twisted with apprehension at the thought.

Carter shoved his phone back into his pocket and got on the elevator, still no sign of Ainsley anywhere.

Just like before, he got off on the fourth floor and walked toward his room.

Should he tell Ainsley about the texts?

Logically, he knew he probably should.

But what if there was any truth to those messages?

Was there something in Ainsley's purse that might make her look guilty?

Or was someone simply messing with Carter's head? And if so, who? Why?

Carter had operated on his own for so long.

But the texts had left him feeling unnerved.

As soon as he stepped inside his room, he spotted Ainsley standing in the entry, staring at him as if she'd been waiting.

"That took longer than I thought," she said. "Haley and I ran out of things to talk about an hour ago. Actually, we never really had anything to talk about from the start."

"Jack, on the other hand, never seems to run out of things to talk about—mostly because he talks about himself." Carter locked the door behind him.

"That sounds about right." A moment of awkward silence fell between them until Ainsley turned and looked around the suite where they were staying.

Though the space was large, it was still one room. Two couches sat in the corner, a kitchenette in another corner, and a king-size bed stretched in the center of it all. The only separate spaces were the bathroom and closet.

"I'll take the couch." Carter nodded toward the furniture.

"Don't be ridiculous. You're the one Jack is courting. I'm just tagging along. I should clearly take the couch and let you enjoy the bed."

"Come on. I'm already emasculated enough by having a female bodyguard."

She raised her eyebrows and crossed her arms as feistiness flashed in her gaze. "Emasculated? I didn't think you were that type."

"You know I try not to have an ego, but . . ."

"Every man has an ego. Every successful man has an even bigger ego."

Carter wanted to argue, but he didn't. He'd met enough people in his line of work to see the truth of those words. He'd like to think he didn't have a big ego, but he didn't have time to dwell on that now.

Instead, he slipped past her. "I'm taking the couch."

Ainsley watched him pass and raised her hands quickly in the air. "Fine. Have it your way."

Carter had a feeling this was just the beginning of the awkwardness that the two of them were bound to experience.

Either way . . . they were essentially trapped here right now and at the mercy of Jack Earl.

They were going to have to learn to get along.

IF AINSLEY COULD HAVE FIGURED out an alternative, she wouldn't be in this suite alone with Carter right now.

They'd successfully pulled off a fake relationship today. But their time together hadn't been pleasant, to say the least. *And* they still needed to get through two full days together.

Carter sat at the desk and opened his laptop, muttering something about answering some emails.

Were they work-related? Or personal?

She wondered a moment about Carter's love life. It wasn't any of her business—except for the fact they were supposed to be married. He'd told Ainsley he was single. But was he really?

Carter was the type of guy who could get whatever girl he wanted.

He'd once wanted her. Or so she'd thought.

Somehow Ainsley had fallen for that whole song and dance.

But she wouldn't make that mistake again.

She sat on the edge of her bed and looked up anything else she could find out about Everett Maurice. The man had dominated Wall Street and the field of finance. He was the investor wealthy people sought after in order to help them grow their wealth even more.

But he'd started as the CFO for NorthStar.

Everett was one more person associated with Jack who had died recently.

That couldn't be a coincidence.

Ainsley just needed to prove it.

As Ainsley sat back in the bed, her thoughts continued to turn over.

What if other people associated with Jack Earl had died, and they hadn't made that connection yet?

And what about Maureen? Was she also connected with Jack?

The possibilities were worth exploring.

She needed to tell Carter about it.

But he seemed deep in thought right now, so she decided to keep doing her online research.

Her gaze lingered on him as he sat at the desk. His muscles looked tight and rigid as he leaned over his computer.

The man was handsome, smart, and successful. He was also well-rounded and could have conversations with anyone. He knew a lot about a lot—which made him handsome, smart, successful, *and* interesting.

At one time, Ainsley had loved listening to him talk about everything he knew. She'd been fascinated by him, really. He'd seen parts of the world she'd only dreamed about visiting. Her life had been mostly limited to Texas.

With a sigh, she lowered her phone and cleared her throat. These thoughts weren't going anywhere good.

"We should probably talk," she announced.

Carter glanced back before turning toward her and releasing a long breath. "Probably."

"Did Jack say anything of use?"

"No, nothing. I'm sorry. I'm not really sure why he insisted on having a 'man talk,' as he called it. It was really quite strange."

She frowned. "At the first indication that I have ulterior motives, he's going to shut down."

"I agree."

Or he would hurt Carter—just like he'd most likely staged the accident that claimed Carter's father's life. Ainsley had no doubt that Jack thought Carter had information left to him by his father. The only way to learn how much he knew was by keeping Carter close.

Plus, his father had been developing that encryption program. If Carter finished what his father had started, then maybe Jack could get his hands on it. Use it to his advantage.

Jack must be dealing with some high-stakes information if he needed to encrypt it that badly.

But Ainsley didn't bring that up. Not yet.

Instead, she told Carter about Everett's death.

Carter's eyes widened as he shook his head. "What? Why haven't I heard anything about this yet? I knew him. He was friends with my father."

Ainsley had seen pictures of Everett and Doyle together. "I'm sorry for your loss."

He squeezed the skin between his eyes. "I can't believe this. First my dad. Then Maureen. Now Everett? This can't be accidental."

"That's what I think also."

"Anyone who crosses Jack seems to end up dead."

"That means we're going to have to be very

careful."

"I agree." Carter sighed and leaned back. "I'm still trying to find out exactly how we're going to get our hands on the information we need. Don't get me wrong, I want to bring this guy down more than anybody. But it's not like Jack is going to openly admit he's doing anything wrong."

"He won't. Ever. But somewhere, somehow there has to be evidence to confirm what he did."

"If there is evidence, it's not likely he brought it with him on a trip." Carter shrugged. "Why would he?"

"It's most likely not something he wants to leave behind either—he'd be too protective of it. Wherever he's keeping this hard drive, he most likely has the device with him. If anyone were to find it, it would nearly be impossible to access the information. As you know, it will be encrypted."

"The perfect way to hide anything of importance." Carter shrugged again.

Whatever that information was, it was serious enough to kill for.

Ainsley didn't like the thought of that.

Before they could talk anymore, their door rattled.

Almost as if someone was trying to get inside.

Ainsley jumped to her feet, preparing herself for the worst.

CHAPTER
EIGHTEEN

AINSLEY peered out the peep hole.

She saw no one.

Gripping her gun, she carefully opened the door.

Carter lingered behind her.

But when she stepped into the hallway, no one was there.

Her back muscles tightened with apprehension.

Was someone playing mind games with them?

With one more glance, she closed the door and double-checked all the locks before walking back toward the bed.

"What was that about?" Carter asked.

Ainsley frowned. "I don't know. Another mind game? An innocent prank by the kids staying down the hallway?"

"I don't know what the outcome of this assignment is going to be, Ainsley," Carter muttered.

She heard the truth in his words. They might not walk away from this.

But there was no fear in his voice—not fear for himself, at least.

"I'm going to do the right thing here, no matter what it cost," she announced.

He stared at her a moment before nodding. "Very well."

She swallowed hard, unsure if she liked the look of admiration in his eyes. Finally, she said, "I say we try to get some sleep."

Carter gave her a look but said nothing.

Then he climbed back under the blankets on the couch.

But an hour later, Ainsley was still lying in bed, unable to sleep.

It had nothing to do with the fact that Carter was in the same room with her.

Yet it had everything to do with the fact that Carter was in the same room with her.

She'd hoped and prayed she'd never see the man again.

Yet here they were.

The last time she'd actually put eyes on him was at her brother's funeral.

She'd seen him from across the room, looking as handsome as ever.

She'd caught him looking at her.

Ainsley had brought her then boyfriend with her.

But her thoughts hadn't really been on her broken heart then. Well, they had been. But her heart had been broken for an entirely different reason.

Her brother—her best friend—had been killed in a terrorist bombing in Florida.

He'd just started working for Texas Senator Leno Hendricks. A different senator—Arnold Velasquez from the Sunshine State—had been killed in a tragic hiking accident, and his colleagues had gathered in Florida on the day before his funeral.

Among those at the funeral was Sheila Soldier, football superstar Benjamin Soldier's mother. She was a lobbyist who'd also come out to show her respects.

Many people in town for the funeral had stayed at that hotel.

While they were sleeping that night, a bomb had exploded and destroyed the whole building.

Jason and Sheila had died with the rest.

More than fourteen years later, Charlie had approached Ainsley and asked her to join the gang at Vanishing Ranch. She'd told Ainsley that she was also investigating what had happened.

Ainsley knew she needed a change—especially after everything she'd had to deal with regarding Dante. She'd jumped on the opportunity.

But she had no idea that meant she'd have to deal with Carter again.

She stared at the man as he lay on the couch, narrowing her eyes at the sight of him.

If putting up with Carter meant she might gain some answers, then it was a sacrifice she was willing to make.

But she wouldn't enjoy it.

———

Carter found it impossible to sleep knowing that Ainsley was in the same room with him. Apparently, she was having trouble resting also because she tossed and turned.

The moment brought back memories of the summer he'd spent at her family's ranch.

One night before Jason left for his internship, he, Ainsley, and Jason had decided to sleep under the stars. They'd had a bonfire and sat around for hours just talking and laughing like they didn't have a care in the world.

In truth, Carter had a lot of cares. It was why he'd come to the ranch for the summer—to get away from the pressures at home. He was an only child, the one on whom his parents had placed all their hopes and dreams.

He hadn't even been sure exactly what he wanted.

Football or a career in the tech field?

He'd eventually chosen the tech field.

Being with Ainsley had brought him so much healing and hope.

Then normal life had resumed, and all that had ended.

He frowned and pressed his head deeper into his pillow.

A moment later, Ainsley threw the covers off of her and tiptoed out of bed.

Carter remained still so she'd think he was sleeping.

She grabbed her phone and quietly opened the door to the balcony. Then she stepped outside, closing the door all but an inch.

Why did she need to make a late-night secret call?

His curiosity piqued.

Unable to stop himself, Carter crept from the bed. He kept his blanket around him as he stepped closer to the door, to the small opening where her voice barely drifted inside.

Maybe he shouldn't listen. But his life was on the

line right now. If Ainsley was hiding something, he deserved to know what it was.

That's when he heard her say, "But if he's still in prison, then . . ."

Ainsley's voice drifted, a tinge of fear woven into her tone.

Was she talking about her stalker? The man who'd left the flowers for her?

Carter's heart pounded as he listened. He knew there was more to that story. He wanted to know what it was. But he also knew it wasn't his business.

As Ainsley's conversation veered into another subject, he stared at her purse as it sat atop the dresser.

What exactly was inside?

He glanced at the door again as he tried to decide if this was his best opportunity to find out.

CHAPTER
NINETEEN

AFTER A MOMENT OF CONTEMPLATION, Carter grabbed Ainsley's purse.

What was he even looking for?

Even if there was nothing incriminating inside, would she ever forgive him?

If there was one thing his mom had taught him, it was to never go through a woman's purse.

But these were extraordinary circumstances.

He prayed he didn't regret this.

Carter rifled through several things—Ainsley's wallet, a hairbrush, some bubble gum.

Tucked into one pocket was a small handgun. That didn't surprise him. He'd seen her with the gun earlier.

Then he felt along the bottom of the purse.

That's when he paused.

Something was nestled beneath the fabric at the bottom.

He reached under the purse's gusset, and his fingers closed over something.

Before he could grasp it, he saw Ainsley's shadow move on the other side of the curtain.

Was she coming back in?

He froze. Waited. Prepared himself to move quickly.

Then she drifted away.

He released his breath and pulled the object out.

When he saw what it was, he sucked in a breath.

Was this a . . . detonator?

Like the one used to set off the bomb that had killed Maureen?

Could Ainsley have been behind it?

His heart pounded harder.

He didn't even want to think about that possibility. It didn't seem real. Yet here was the evidence.

Had the device been planted here?

He didn't know.

As he saw the shadow moving closer again, he quickly shoved the detonator back into her purse and placed the bag on the dresser where he'd found it.

He slipped under the blankets on the couch and stilled just as the door opened.

He was just in time.

Ainsley slipped back inside.

But Carter could feel the secrets and tension floating between them like a ticking time bomb.

Should he confront her?

Or did he have more power knowing the device was there while Ainsley thought her secret was safe?

———

Ainsley awoke the next morning still feeling out of sorts.

Her phone call last night with Charlie hadn't made her feel any better.

Ainsley had hoped her boss would have better news. What exactly did better news look like? She wasn't sure.

But there were no updates on Maureen's death. The police were still looking into it. They'd reviewed the neighbor's security videos, which hadn't shown anything—not even someone leaving a rose on Ainsley's SUV.

Charlie had one of their guys looking into Maureen's past for any specific reason she would be targeted. Most likely, she'd been killed to send a message to Carter. But they didn't know that for sure yet.

Then Charlie had told her that Dante was still behind bars.

Ainsley didn't necessarily want him to be out. But that theory was the only thing that had made sense.

If Dante wasn't leaving those flowers for her, then who was?

Ainsley couldn't let herself be distracted. She had to be vigilant. Her first priority was keeping an eye on Carter.

Speaking of Carter . . . the man was already awake and in the bathroom. She heard the water running on the other side of the wall.

She let out a deep breath and stood, pulling on a robe the lodge had provided over the T-shirt and shorts she'd slept in.

Slipping the gun into her pocket, she walked toward the door and opened it.

A newspaper waited there.

Every morning, she read the paper while she drank her coffee so she could stay informed—a trait that had been ingrained in her by her father.

None of those digital newspapers would do either. Only in a bind.

As she reached down and grabbed it, the door across the hall opened.

Ainsley stiffened and started to reach for her gun, expecting the worst.

When she looked up, she spotted Hayes.

Good. He was staying close. That knowledge made her feel a little better.

The two exchanged a nod before Hayes grabbed his own paper and stepped back into his room.

Ainsley slipped back into her room and locked the door. When she got to the coffee maker, she noted that Carter had already started a pot.

That was something she could get used to.

But she wouldn't.

The man's face drifted through her mind again, and Ainsley frowned.

At one time, she'd daydreamed about that face day in and day out. Carter had been her first crush. Her first heartbreak. Her first realization that men—other than her dad and brother—couldn't be trusted.

She'd proceeded with caution ever since then.

She had dated from time to time. But no one seriously.

Then Dante had drifted into her life and messed her up even more.

Now, Ainsley was trying to be content with her job.

She glanced at the time. She and Carter only had forty minutes until they had to meet the rest of the crew. Hopefully, Carter would be done soon so she could get ready.

In the meantime, she opened the paper to scan the headlines.

The breath left her lungs.

Tucked between the pages were photos.

Photos of her, Carter, Haley, and Jack having dinner last night. Another photo of Ainsley having coffee with Haley. Another of Ainsley and Carter with their arms around each other as they faked their romance.

Someone clearly wanted to make a statement.

A statement that she was being watched.

It was only a matter of time before this person revealed his plan.

If this was Dante, then that plan would be deadly.

However, he was in prison, Ainsley reminded herself.

But what if he'd recruited someone else to do his dirty work?

CHAPTER
TWENTY

WITH CARTER still in the bathroom, Ainsley grabbed her purse to pull out some lip balm.

As she fished through her bag, she felt something on the bottom—something that hadn't been there before.

She paused, and her muscles stiffened.

Carefully, she pulled the object out.

It was . . . a detonator.

The breath left her lungs.

A detonator?

How had that gotten in her purse?

Her heart pounded harder as she stared at it.

She never left her purse unattended. But she supposed someone skilled enough could have dropped this inside. It was heavy enough it would have fallen to the bottom where she'd found it.

But why? Why would someone leave this here?

Unless they wanted to set her up.

Her heart continued to slam into her ribcage.

Her hands trembled as she called Charlie to tell her about it. Should she go to the police with this? Sit on it? Was this the detonator connected with Maureen's death?

"Just stay calm," Charlie said. "Leave it in your room—under your mattress. I'll tell Hayes to get it after you leave. We'll test it. I don't want to raise any alarms if it's not necessary. Someone could just be trying to shake you up."

It was working.

Ainsley stared at the bathroom door. What if Carter found out about this? He'd really never trust her if he learned she had it.

"Charlie . . . someone must know who I am," Ainsley muttered. "Why I'm here. They left pictures in my newspaper this morning. Surveillance-like pictures of me and Carter. If someone is on to us, that could put our whole plan in jeopardy."

"I agree that things are getting dicey. The key question is: Does Jack know who you are?"

"He hasn't given an indication."

"It's your call, Ainsley. But if he's not suspicious, I'd stay put. This is our one opportunity to find out what we need."

"I agree. I'll . . . I'll do what I can."

"Remember—we have intel that Jack takes a hard drive of information wherever he goes—almost as if it were his family's crown jewels or something. Brody gave you that device that's set up to copy Jack's data. That's all you need to do. Copy the drive and get out. There's no need to confront anyone."

"Does Carter know that?" His face flashed in her mind.

"He should. But be careful. I don't like this."

Neither did Ainsley.

———

Carter tried to calm the tremor of nerves raking through him as he and Ainsley took the stairs down to meet Jack and the gang.

But all he could think about was that detonator.

Should he confront Ainsley?

Go to the police?

He still wasn't sure.

Whatever move he made, he had to be sure it was the right one.

The group had already gathered in the lobby, and he could hear jovial laughs escaping from them as they waited.

They were the type of people with big personalities, who needed others to notice them in order to feel important.

Carter had been around these kinds of people many times before and could read them like a book.

Jack might be powerful, but there were still insecurities lingering in the depths of his gaze—insecurities that fueled his need for attention and validation. Plus, he had that unquenchable thirst for more.

Carter had read a profile on him once. He knew that Jack had grown up with nothing and had eventually built an empire. Did Jack feel a desperate need to prove himself?

He wasn't sure.

As soon as Jack saw them, he turned to them with a wide grin and clapped his hands. "If it isn't the man of the hour and his lovely wife."

Carter grinned, trying to seem like a good sport.

But the last thing he'd ever do was work for Jack Earl.

No one else had seemed to suspect that the man was responsible for his father's death. Not the police or FBI. No one else in his family. Not even when Carter had presented his own research to them.

But when Charlie had told him she'd reached the same conclusion, Carter had known he needed to do something. He'd found an ally to work with.

That had led him to this moment.

It had also brought Ainsley back into his life.

He cast that thought aside and instead focused on finding some answers.

Two other men were with Jack . . . Larson Reinhold and Bill "Prancer" Roxboro, as they'd been introduced. Larson was short, balding, and uptight. Prancer was tall and thin with thick dark hair and a quick smile.

Haley was there as well as two other women: Joy and Brooke.

The women were more like trophies than anything else. Of course, some people might say the same thing about Ainsley when they saw her on Carter's arm.

But Ainsley was nothing like these women. She was down-to-earth and not afraid to get dirty or to work hard. She knew who she was, and she wasn't afraid to go for her dreams. She definitely didn't want to ride anybody else's coattails.

She was one of a kind.

A strange ache filled Carter's chest at the thought.

Then he remembered the detonator he'd found in her purse.

Was Ainsley the same person he remembered? Or had she become someone else entirely? He'd seen it happen before. It wasn't out of the realm of possibility.

After a few minutes of chitchat, Jack clapped his hands to get everyone's attention. "We have a great day planned. I've reserved the hot springs just for our group this morning. Following that, we'll have brunch. Then it will be off to the steam room for the menfolk and the spa for these lovely ladies."

Carter listened with interest. It sounded like a full day—a day where Jack Earl tried to prove to Carter that joining together in business would make his life much better—and richer.

"Eric, my assistant, has everything scheduled for us." Jack nodded to a man in the distance.

Carter glanced at him a moment, wondering if he was connected with all this.

"I want us all to have a great time and get to know each other," Jack continued.

That sounded good to Carter—well, maybe not the great time part.

But he'd come to find answers, and that's exactly what he intended to do.

He needed to get his hands on Jack Earl's hard drive. That was his best chance of finding the information he needed.

But he had a feeling that wasn't going to be easy.

CHAPTER
TWENTY-ONE

AINSLEY PAUSED by the hot spring-fed pool.

She didn't want to be impressed.

But the area was breathtaking.

Steam rose from blue-green waters. In the background, snowcapped mountains stretched high into a bright sky. Numerous servers waited nearby to take care of their every whim.

This place and situation were totally out of her league, like something she would see in a movie.

She felt a hand at her waist and flinched—before quickly scolding herself.

She *had* to watch her reactions.

Carter leaned closer, as if about to whisper sweet nothings in her ear. Instead, he whispered, "Don't look so tense."

She giggled and moved closer to him. "Sorry about that, *boo bear*."

He gave her a look.

Good. That's what she'd been going for.

But any humor quickly disappeared as she scanned everything around them one more time.

This wasn't the safest place for them. They were too exposed out here. She'd need to be on guard.

And was she imagining things or was Carter acting funny this morning? More distant—as if that were possible?

She wasn't sure.

She'd have to deal with that later.

"Everyone in!" Jack called. "The water stays about one hundred degrees year-round."

To Ainsley, this was such a strange way to conduct a business meeting. How many people wanted to be in their bathing suits among future colleagues?

Or maybe she was the one out of touch.

When she saw the tiny bikinis the other women wore, she felt overdressed for the occasion.

Either way, she slipped off the plush robe she'd been given and ran a hand over the navy-blue tankini she'd donned. The suit was cute but modest.

She glanced at Carter and saw him quickly look away.

She tried to do the same for him. But her gaze lingered a moment too long on his fit, well-cared-for physique.

As her throat went dry, she averted her gaze.

There was no reason to stare at his six-pack abs—no professional reason, at least.

As the wind blew, goosebumps danced across her skin, reminding her they were in the mountains. Secluded. At the mercy of Jack Earl.

Her purse—with her gun—was in a locker and out of reach.

Carter took her hand and led her into the steaming water.

The warmth instantly relaxed her.

The group of eight all gravitated toward a circular ledge cut out in one of the corners.

It was time to get down to business.

As Ainsley glanced at Carter again, she realized it would be much harder to stay focused than she'd assumed.

Above all, she had to keep her eyes open for danger.

Carter didn't want to feel awkward as he sat on the ledge beside Ainsley.

But he did.

Especially as Haley lingered behind Jack, rubbing his shoulders, and the other two couples flirted and clung to each other.

Then there was him and Ainsley. They could fake *some* affection. But they were otherwise out of their element here. Even if they were dating or married, he wouldn't be all over her while out in public.

He watched as Jack laughed, acting like the king of his domain, as dainty snowflakes fell all around them. The snow would be good for the slopes, but not as good for the roads—especially if it was as heavy as forecasters predicted.

This man thought he was untouchable, didn't he?

Carter's gut clenched in anger at the thought.

"I know I've already said this, but I was so sorry to hear about your dad." Jack's expression sobered. "He was a brilliant man."

Carter drew in a deep breath as he tried to refocus his thoughts. "He was. His death was a huge loss— not only to my family, but to the technology industry as a whole."

"I agree." Jack shifted, his arms casually draped on the edge of the pool. "I understand you have your father's smarts. Everyone speaks highly of you. Some have even said you're more brilliant than your dad.

That software you developed set you up for life, didn't it?"

Carter shrugged. "I don't know if I'd say I'm more brilliant than my father. But I'm good at what I do."

"Tell me—did your dad teach you everything he knew?"

Carter swallowed hard.

This was the rub.

The real reason Jack wanted him here.

What had his dad discovered—or created—that left Jack feeling so threatened?

Carter was determined to get to the bottom of it.

He released a long breath. "Everything he knew? He was too smart for that. Besides, he thought he had more time. His death was so sudden and unexpected."

But Carter had noticed his dad acting strangely in the weeks before the supposed accident. He'd asked him about it once. His father had brushed him off, said there was nothing to worry about.

Why hadn't his father told him if something was going on? Carter could have helped.

What had his dad known that had ultimately gotten him killed?

That was the question Carter needed answered.

Whatever that information was, it could give Jack even more power.

Or it might have the power to ruin the man. Maybe to ruin other powerful people also. After all, Jack was a close friend with former president Bill Radar.

More so, did this somehow tie in with what happened with Charlie's father, Benjamin Soldier?

CHAPTER
TWENTY-TWO

AINSLEY SNUGGLED AGAINST CARTER, trying to look natural and in love.

At least, the conversation was finally going somewhere.

But it would be hard to find out any answers if they didn't blend in. They couldn't let any opportunity slip by.

With that thought, Ainsley tilted her head and placed a few lingering kisses on Carter's neck.

He stiffened for a moment, then tugged her closer.

Jack's gaze took in every movement, and a smug smile crossed his features.

"How did you know Carter's father, Jack?" Ainsley asked.

"We worked together on a few projects. I knew

from the moment I met him that I wanted him on my team. Same for Carter. I asked him to come aboard earlier, but he declined. Since I'm not one to take no for an answer, I thought I'd keep trying until my persistence pays off."

Ainsley was sure he thought he'd get his way. Jack *expected* his persistence to pay off. He was that kind of guy.

As the conversation continued, she scanned everything around them.

A man lingering on the other side of the expansive patio caught her eye.

He wasn't dressed as an employee of the resort. The other employees wore matching white puffy jackets and black pants. This guy wore a black jacket and jeans.

Ainsley's muscles tightened.

Jack had said he'd reserved this time just for his group.

What was this other guy doing here?

Was he the man who'd left the roses and pictures?

Or maybe Jack had his own guys keeping an eye on them.

She didn't know.

But she didn't feel comfortable knowing he was out there.

The man saw Ainsley looking at him and disappeared inside the lodge.

If she wanted to catch this guy, she didn't have much time.

She rose, the sudden action causing everyone to turn toward her. "I'm feeling a little queasy. It's probably the altitude. If you'll excuse me a moment, I'm going to grab some water and take a quick breather."

"Of course," Jack said. "Drink a lot of water. You'll thank me for it later!"

Carter's gaze lingered on her, full of questions.

But she couldn't explain now.

Instead, Ainsley quickly grabbed her robe and slipped inside, hoping to find the man she'd just seen.

———

"I hope she's okay," Jack muttered, following Ainsley with his eyes as she left the hot springs.

Carter forced his gaze away, hoping the same thing. "She gets a bit of altitude sickness, apparently."

"Apparently?" Larson raised an eyebrow.

Carter shrugged. "We had a bit of a whirlwind romance and marriage. So we're still learning a lot about each other."

"Hope you signed a prenup," Prancer said with a

knowing laugh.

Carter returned the laugh, leaving it up to the man to assume whether he did or not. Personally, if he didn't trust a woman enough to marry her without a prenup, then he knew he shouldn't marry her.

As the conversation continued, Carter tried not to think about Ainsley. But if she'd left, she'd had a good reason.

Had she seen something?

The only thing that made him feel better was knowing she could defend herself.

However, her gun was tucked away in a locker and out of reach right now.

Trepidation grew inside him.

Carter turned back to Jack, determined to finish this conversation. "I was watching TV the other day, and I thought I saw something about you and President Radar meeting."

Jack grinned. "Guilty as charged."

"You have some amazing connections."

"Sometimes business is all about having the right contacts."

There was something about this man Carter didn't like. Didn't trust. But he'd known that before coming on this trip.

Jack Earl was the kind of guy who looked out for

his own interests.

What Carter wasn't sure about was what this man was covering up.

Carter had already gone through some of his father's files, looking for anything his dad may have discovered that might have gotten his dad killed.

But within hours of his father's death, his computer had been wiped clean.

Carter had been able to get beyond several firewalls and save some information before it totally disappeared.

But what he'd found had only left him with more questions and no more answers. There had been a list of names—though none of them appeared to be real persons. They were placeholders or code names. He wasn't sure which.

There were dates and times and locations listed with each name.

But no pertinent information.

Carter had a feeling what he'd found had been a rough draft of information or an outline of sorts.

The final details had probably been tucked away somewhere even safer, somewhere with even more firewalls. Possibly encrypted with this new tech.

Whatever Jack was hiding, it was serious.

Worth killing for.

They had to find out what it was.

TWENTY-THREE

AINSLEY SLIPPED inside the building and glanced around.

Where had that man gone?

She hadn't gotten a good look at his face. She'd only noticed the black jacket he was wearing.

But he couldn't have gotten far.

Moving quickly, she headed toward the opposite side of the lobby surrounding the hot springs. Several doors led off into other rooms. Two led to the locker rooms and two to the restrooms. There was also an office and a storage area for towels.

A thirty-something woman with a puckered face stepped in front of Ainsley as she headed toward the locker rooms. "Can I help you? Anything you need, I'm here for you."

Ainsley resisted the urge to push the woman out

of her way. That wouldn't be polite. But she didn't have time for a long, drawn-out conversation either.

"I saw a man come this way," Ainsley said. "I thought I recognized him from my days back at Texas State. Did you see him by chance? He's a tall guy with a black jacket."

The woman shook her head. "I'm sorry. I haven't seen anyone other than the employees here and your group in the pool. Are you enjoying yourself?"

This was the long, drawn-out conversation Ainsley had hoped to avoid.

"Yes, but I'm just going to slip down that hallway and see if I can spot him. It's going to drive me crazy unless I find out. You know how that goes sometimes?"

The woman let out a quick, uptight laugh. "Of course. I won't hold you up anymore."

With that, Ainsley hurried away.

As she stepped into the hallway, she glanced back and forth but saw no one.

That man hadn't disappeared into thin air.

But she wasn't sure she would be able to search for him right now without raising a lot of questions.

That wasn't what she wanted.

She could feel defeat pressing on her.

She hadn't expected to find answers quickly. But

she also hadn't expected things to accelerate as they had.

Ainsley could feel the danger in the air, and she knew she needed to be more vigilant than ever.

———

Carter glanced back at the door where Ainsley had disappeared.

Was she okay? How long would she be gone?

"Early on during my first marriage, I hated being away from my wife for more than five minutes," Larson said. "I can see that in you also."

Carter turned back to the group, his throat tightening. "Maybe it's the curse of being a newlywed."

"Enjoy it while it lasts." Prancer grinned. "How many marriages do we have collectively? Eight?"

The men chuckled.

Carter shrugged, refusing to find that number amusing. "I believe marriage is for life, so I plan on this being my only one."

He swallowed after making the statement. He hadn't meant for that to escape. But his words were true. So many people treated marriage like buying a new car. Once you got tired of the vehicle you had, you traded it in for a shiny new model.

That wasn't what Carter believed, however.

Still, he and Ainsley weren't really married so his words felt like a lie.

"Either way—I hope both of you enjoy your time here." Jack gave a pointed look to his colleagues. Clearly, the man didn't want anything to be said that might dissuade Carter from coming onboard.

However, it would be hard to enjoy anything considering the fact Ainsley couldn't stand him. Even though sixteen years had passed, it didn't seem as if much had changed between them.

It probably didn't matter anymore anyway. Too much time had gone by. Too much history.

That history was a bit like cement. It had started as soft and pliable. But as more time passed, it hardened into a more permanent fixture—a wall that couldn't be crossed.

Ainsley still didn't want to listen to his explanation.

He *would* like to hear her explanation, however. He wanted to know what that detonator was doing in her purse.

Carter still hadn't decided how to handle that situation.

But he needed to decide soon.

TWENTY-FOUR

CARTER FELT relief wash through him when Ainsley finally returned to the hot springs.

She looked unharmed as she paused near the water. She started to take her robe off when Jack stopped her.

"It's almost time for our brunch, so why don't we all take a few minutes to get ready? There's no need to look fancy or get dressed up. But brunch will be served in thirty minutes in my private dining hall—The Aspen. Does everyone think they can work with that?"

Murmurs of affirmation went through the group.

Carter climbed out and grabbed his robe. He was anxious to hear what had just happened. Was Ainsley up to something? He hated to wonder that—but he had to be smart here.

He took Ainsley's hand, noting how natural it felt to feel their fingers intertwined. And when Ainsley turned and wrapped her arms around his neck, all the air left his lungs.

This isn't real, he reminded himself. None of it.

She leaned close until her breath tickled his ear. "I thought I saw someone, but he got away."

Alarm raced through him. "Someone?"

"I'm not sure who, but he was watching us. I needed to make sure you were safe."

Carter's stomach clenched. That *he* was safe? He hardly even cared about his own safety. He just needed to know Ainsley would be okay.

Memories flashed back to him.

Memories of one of the rodeos Ainsley had been in.

One of the guys she'd been competing against didn't like that Ainsley had won what he considered to be his rightful title a few weeks earlier. The man definitely didn't like losing to a woman. So he'd sent some of his friends to scare her off.

Carter had walked in just as they'd surrounded her in a horse stall.

He'd lost a tooth during the fistfight that broke out.

But Ainsley had been kept safe.

The other bull rider had been arrested.

And Ainsley had gone on to win again.

Carter would take a fist to his face any time if it meant standing up for her.

He would tell her that, but he was sure that wouldn't make a difference. Ainsley was solely focused right now on her assignment.

Besides, he really needed to keep her at arm's length. He was usually so good at separating his personal life and business. But this was proving to be difficult.

"How are you handling all this?" Ainsley whispered.

He glanced around him at Jack's group. "I don't like these people."

"Neither do I. But we can get through this together. Okay?"

Carter liked the confidence in Ainsley's voice. Liked the feeling of her arms around his neck. Liked how her breaths tickled his hair.

But the stakes were rising.

As much as he'd like to believe that two days would be enough to find the information he needed, he wasn't sure if that was true or not.

Ainsley leaned closer and whispered, "I checked my phone while I was gone. I got a message saying that Everett Maurice had a meeting the day before he died."

"A meeting with who?"

Ainsley pulled back enough to look him in the eye. "Prancer."

Carter bit down. Another suspect.

What if Jack wasn't the one behind this?

What if it was someone else here at this resort?

He didn't know who to trust . . . even when it came to Ainsley.

He had to ask her about that detonator. He had to know if he could trust her.

Because, if he couldn't, he needed to send her back to Arizona.

———

Brunch—which included caviar and truffles—had been delicious but uneventful.

Ainsley had kept her eyes open for anyone suspicious.

She'd seen no one.

However, they were in an enclosed room with no windows.

She'd managed to eat a few things to make sure she kept her energy steady.

But the conversation mostly revolved around the stock market—something she had no interest in and that didn't seem to tie in with this case.

When the subject of how a certain stock had "bombed" came up, she saw Carter's gaze darken.

Was he thinking about Maureen?

When they finished, Jack announced it was time for the women to head to the spa while the men went to the steam room.

Ainsley would prefer that the group stay together, but she knew she couldn't raise a fuss.

Instead, she nodded and smiled as if delighted to be pampered.

Before they split, Carter pulled her aside.

His gaze looked stormy, and she braced herself for whatever he might have to say.

"There's been something on my mind that I need to ask you about," Carter said. "I wanted to wait. But now I realize that I can't. I can't work with you if I don't know if I can trust you."

"What are you talking about?"

"I know about the detonator in your purse."

Ainsley sucked in a breath. "What?"

"Don't deny it."

"I won't. But I didn't put it there. I don't know who did. And how did you even know about it?"

He ignored her question. "Where is it now?"

"Hayes has it, and he's checking it out. Someone planted it there."

Carter stared at her another moment as if he didn't know whether or not to believe her.

"Do you always go through women's purses?" Ainsley finally asked.

A flush of embarrassment swept over him. "No, as a matter of fact, I don't."

"So . . ." She had a feeling there was more to this story.

His embarrassment turned into a scowl. "Someone texted me and told me to look."

"What?" Her question came out louder than she intended.

Carter looked around before nodding. "This person has texted me twice. Both times about you."

Her eyes widened with surprise. "Why didn't you tell me?"

"Because I didn't know if I could trust you."

"What have *I* ever done to make *you* doubt that you could trust *me*?"

They stared off for another moment before Jack called for Carter, breaking the fragile tension stretching between them.

AINSLEY TOOK one last look at Carter as he left with the rest of the guys.

She couldn't get their conversation out of her mind.

Someone *wanted* to turn Carter against her.

Someone knew more about her than she was comfortable with.

Ainsley knew she had to be willing to pull the plug at the first sign things were going south. But for now, she didn't think Carter was in danger. He probably wouldn't be until he started asking probing questions.

Still, Ainsley preferred to remain close to him—especially if she was supposed to protect him. It would be hard to do that while she was at the spa and he was in the steam room. At least, she'd seen

Hayes lingering nearby. She had no doubt he'd find a way to stay near Carter.

Ainsley lifted up a prayer for Carter's safety.

Hayes had texted her earlier. He'd managed to check the security footage outside her room. A bellhop had left both the rose and the newspaper. Hayes had talked to the man, and he'd claimed a guest asked him to leave those things for Ainsley. The bellhop said that man seemed nice and that he'd wanted to surprise Ainsley.

Hayes had a description. The guy was tall with dark hair. He wore a baseball cap and an oversized sweatshirt.

In other words, it had been hard to make out any fine details.

However, Ainsley would keep that description in the back of her mind.

Dante was on the shorter side with a round face.

But he could have an accomplice.

Her throat tightened at the thought.

Too many questions circled in her head.

Meanwhile, the ladies looped arms with each other as they started toward the spa . . .

Ainsley joined them, plastering on a bubbly smile.

She would act her way through this.

But a bad feeling brewed in her gut.

Carter leaned against the wall as steam hung in the air around him.

Sweat covered his body.

Was this really good for you? That's what people said.

But he had his doubts.

"So, Carter . . ." Jack started. "As you know, we're hoping you'll join our team at NorthStar. We wanted to give you the chance to meet a few key players at the company and get a feel for us and what we do. What are you thinking about that opportunity now? We could really use someone with your skillset."

He adjusted the towel around his waist. "I'm honored that you're considering me. As you know, I've been an independent contractor for the last few years, working on whatever projects I see fit."

"That sounds like a nice life," Prancer said. "But not as nice as the one we can offer."

"I'm sure there are a lot of people who could do this job. Why me?"

"I beg to differ with that assessment," Jack said. "It's widely known that you're one of the best cryptographers around—just like your father. We want you on our team. Our social media is being threatened more and more, often by outside forces. That threat is only going to grow as hackers get smarter and smarter."

"What do you think I can help you do?" Carter kept his voice even, but he really wanted to get out of here. It was hard to breathe in all this steam.

"We'd like you to design a program to keep people's information safe," Larson stated.

"And would this program be proprietary?"

"If you worked for us, whatever you did would become the property of NorthStar, of course." Jack flashed a smile. "We have that policy for all our employees. We can't have people selling technology that we paid to have developed, after all."

Carter's throat tightened. "Makes sense. It's definitely something to consider."

"Your father began doing some work for us. With his sudden death, he wasn't able to finish it. In fact, he kept most of his research in some encrypted files."

Was that what this was about? Was there some kind of information hidden in those files that Jack needed?

Carter knew one thing for sure. Once Jack had his hands on whatever it was he wanted, Carter would be as good as dead.

He had no doubt about that.

CHAPTER
TWENTY-SIX

AFTER MUCH DEBATING, the women had decided to do body wraps. Apparently, they helped detoxify your body and took off several inches in the process.

Ainsley *really* wasn't looking forward to this.

But at least she got to wear a bathing suit. That would make this experience a little less awkward.

She expected all of the women to be in the same room for their treatments, which she hoped to use to her advantage. She could ask questions, maybe find out more information on Jack and his associates.

So far, all their conversations had just been painfully superficial—except for one comment by Brooke about a conference taking place in Dallas next month. Business leaders from around the world would be meeting there.

Was this the event where someone planned another terrorist act?

It seemed like a possibility.

Ainsley wasn't sure what to expect from this treatment, but she would just try to make the best of it.

However, when they were called back, each woman was led to a separate room, and Ainsley's hopes of asking Brooke more about the conference plummeted.

Ainsley followed her technician—a thirty-something woman dressed in khakis and a white shirt, who'd introduced herself as Katie—into a dimly lit room with soft harp music playing in the background and the scent of essential oils floating in the air.

Ainsley was instructed to slip out of her robe and lie on a heated blanket to begin the treatment.

So far so good.

"Just try to relax," Katie said as she rubbed Ainsley's shoulders.

If only she could . . .

She glanced at her purse resting on the table against the wall, knowing her gun was inside. All she had to do was reach three feet and grab it if anyone threatened her.

Still, her gut twisted with unease.

Katie began pulling out heated cloths that had

been saturated in tea leaves and essential oils that smelled like lemon and orange. She draped them across Ainsley.

The warmth felt good.

But Ainsley was still having trouble unwinding. Too much was going on. Too much was at stake.

"How long have you worked here?" she asked Katie.

"About four months."

"Have you met Jack Earl yet?"

Katie smiled and placed another wrap over Ainsley. "I have. He's larger than life, isn't he?"

"Does he come here a lot?" Sweat beaded across her forehead, and this wrap was seeming like a worse and worse idea all the time.

Plus, there was another smell in here she couldn't identify. Maybe it was some kind of essential oil they used for the weight loss portion of the wrap. Ainsley wasn't sure.

But she didn't like it.

"Every couple of weeks," Katie said, her voice calm and soothing.

"Is that right?" Ainsley tried to process that. Did Jack conduct a lot of business here? Maybe if she could find out who he was meeting with . . .

She started to ask the question, but her head began to swim.

Was it the heat? Was her body having some type of allergic reaction to the essential oils?

Ainsley started to ask if she was supposed to feel this way. But before she could, Katie took the blankets Ainsley lay on and wrapped them around her until she felt like a mummy.

Worse yet, her arms were trapped inside.

"Ma'am . . ." Ainsley muttered, her words slurring slightly.

Katie barely seemed to hear her as she continued to wrap Ainsley tighter.

Ainsley's lungs constricted. Her head swam.

What was wrong with her?

She had no idea.

Panic surged through her.

She had to get out of this cocoon she'd been wrapped in.

Her life depended on it.

———

Carter got dressed after they finished in the steam room, happy to have that experience over with. He didn't feel like he could breathe in there. How did Jack and his crew do that all the time?

Then he wandered back to the lobby where they had all planned to meet.

The other guys had decided to stop by the bar to grab a quick drink before meeting back up with the women.

But he was anxious to see Ainsley.

As he glanced around, he saw the other three women waiting.

But no Ainsley.

"What did you guys do with my wife?" Carter tried to keep his voice light as he paused in front of them. "Am I going to recognize her when I see her again?"

Haley offered a cunning grin. "She left the spa before the rest of us."

"Really? That doesn't sound like Ainsley." His throat tightened, though he told himself to hold his concerns at bay.

"That's what the woman at the spa's front desk said." Haley shrugged as if she didn't have a care in the world.

She glanced at Brooke and Joy, and they nodded in agreement.

Carter's shoulders tensed.

Something wasn't right. If Ainsley had left early, she would have come looking for him. She wasn't the type to wander off.

"Maybe she went back to the spa for some reason," Carter said. "I'm going to see if I can find her. Which way to the spa?"

Brooke pointed in the correct direction.

Carter took off toward it, hating the apprehension he felt. He kept his steps slow as to not raise anyone's suspicions.

He'd spotted Hayes several times today, keeping an eye on him from a distance.

But who was keeping an eye on Ainsley?

Once Carter was around the corner and out of sight, he picked up his pace. He quickly tried Ainsley's phone as he dashed toward the spa.

She didn't answer.

More apprehension raced up his spine.

He burst into the spa and rushed toward the front desk. The woman behind it appeared startled as her eyes widened and shoulders tensed.

"I'm trying to find my wife. Ainsley Winslow." He had to admit that the name had a nice ring to it—if only he was a believer of unreasonable dreams.

Taking all the time in the world, the receptionist—Greta, her nametag read—glanced at her appointment book before shaking her head. "Mrs. Winslow's appointment was two hours ago. She should be done."

"I know. But that's why I'm here. No one has seen her."

Greta looked at the book again before shaking her

head. "I'm sorry. She should've left at least twenty minutes ago."

Carter took a deep breath, trying to keep his panic under control.

He thanked the woman before stepping away and pulling out his phone.

He tried to call Ainsley again, but she didn't answer.

He hoped he was overreacting, but he didn't think he was. Just to be certain he wasn't overlooking something, he quickly checked the restrooms—both in the spa and in the lobby.

She wasn't there.

Carter needed to call Hayes. Ainsley had texted him the man's number last night.

Hayes answered on the first ring. "What's going on?"

Carter lowered his voice. "I don't know where Ainsley is, and I'm worried."

"What? Where was she seen the last time?"

"The spa. They said she's not here anymore. But she's not with the other women."

Hayes grumbled something beneath his breath before saying, "I'll be there in two minutes."

But Carter feared they didn't have that much time to waste.

TWENTY-SEVEN

AINSLEY FELT the sweat all over her body. Felt her throat tightening. Her head swirling.

Her mind felt so messed up that she couldn't even think clearly about how to get out of the situation.

She fought against the cloths around her, but it did no good.

They were too tight. She was too weak.

She'd been drugged.

Whatever was on this fabric wasn't just a weight loss formula or toxin cleanser.

Someone had put something more potent on the cloths.

Was one of the other women responsible? They'd been the ones to suggest doing body wraps. They'd even seemed chummy with the people working in the spa.

Everything blurred around her.

As it did, Ainsley felt arms reach beneath her.

Felt herself being lifted and carried.

She glanced back at her purse.

Her gun and her phone were inside.

But she could barely make the shape of it out on the table.

Someone was taking her away from those things —her safety net.

Maybe it didn't matter. She didn't think she could operate either one even if she was holding them.

"Where are you taking me?" she muttered, her words slurring.

"Away from here," the man replied.

Her lungs froze.

Did she recognize that voice?

She blinked, trying to make out the man's features.

But he wore a medical mask and had some type of cloth over his head.

She couldn't see who he was.

She only knew that something was very, very wrong.

If someone was desperate enough to go to these

extremes in order to take her out, then Ainsley was in serious trouble.

———

Carter couldn't wait any longer.

Something was definitely wrong. He had to find Ainsley.

Now.

He rushed back up to Greta at the reception desk. "I need to see the room where she got her wrap."

"Excuse me?" She stared at him blankly.

"I need to see the room where my wife was receiving her spa treatment."

She let out a nervous laugh. "I'm sorry. That's not going to be possible. Someone else is in there now."

"Then I need to see her locker. I need proof that she's not here anymore."

"Sir—"

"Don't sir me." Carter didn't like to use this harsh tone, but he would in desperate situations. This felt like a desperate situation. "I came here as a personal friend of Jack Earl."

Greta's eyes widened at the name drop.

But Carter continued. "She was last seen here, she's no longer with her friends, and she's not answering her phone. You either let me see her locker and the room where she was, or I call the authorities."

"Of course." Greta looked at something else in her appointment book before rising and grabbing some keys. "This way."

She led him into a locker room, clearing it first of any women. Then Greta went to a locker and unlocked it.

Ainsley's clothes were still inside.

Carter's apprehension grew stronger.

"She wouldn't have left this place without her clothes. Believe me. She's very modest." Those words were true.

It was one other thing that Carter had always liked about Ainsley. She didn't feel the need to flaunt just how beautiful she was. Her beauty spoke for itself.

For the first time, Greta actually looked confused also. "I don't understand . . . the book said she was gone. That her bill was comped by Mr. Earl. I just started my shift. I wasn't here when she and her friends left."

"Who was?"

"Kathy. She's already gone for the day."

"We may need to call her. But for right now, I

need to see the room where Ainsley received her treatment—and talk to the employee who was with her."

He wasn't taking no for an answer.

"YOU HAVE to understand that I can't just let you barge in there," Greta said. "There are privacy issues."

"Check to see if anyone is inside," Carter insisted as he stood in the hallway. "Then I'm going in."

Greta frowned. "I understand, but I'm going to have to get my manager involved—"

"We don't have any time to waste." Carter grabbed her arm and stared her in the eye, desperate to get through to her. "Please. This is my wife. We've only been married eight days. I think something's happened to her." His voice cracked.

He wasn't faking his concern. He truly was worried about Ainsley.

Finally, Greta's features softened as understanding seemed to roll over her.

She nodded, her neck stiff as if she were still uncomfortable with all of this. "Let's go."

Carter followed her down the hallway to room eight and waited while she knocked on the door.

When no one answered, she opened it. A knot of confusion twisted between her brows. "No one's here. I don't know why. The book said someone else is supposed to be receiving a treatment in here now."

Carter looked inside, and sure enough, the space was empty.

Except for Ainsley's purse on a counter—probably sitting right where she'd left it.

His heart pounded harder.

He didn't know what was happening. He only knew that Ainsley needed help.

Carter had to figure out how he would give it to her.

———

Ainsley tried to move.

But she couldn't.

Everything blurred around her until she didn't even know where she was.

She hated this helpless feeling.

She knew she was in trouble.

Knew by the time someone found her that it would probably be too late.

Was Dante behind this?

No, Dante was still in prison. That was what Charlie had said.

If not Dante, then who? Did he have an accomplice?

Was Jack suspicious about Ainsley's true identity? Was he trying to off her already?

No, she and Carter had been careful.

None of this made sense.

She tried to speak, to protest.

But only a moan escaped.

A man still carried her.

Down the dark hallway.

He shifted her in his arms.

A door opened then shut.

Then it was cold.

And bright.

"Almost there," the man muttered.

Did she recognize that voice?

She wasn't sure.

What was he going to do with her?

She didn't even want to think about it.

Finally, he opened the door into another room and laid her on the floor.

She still couldn't move. One of the drugs in these wraps must be a sedative.

"I'll be back for you soon," the man muttered. "Sleep tight."

Then the door closed again.

Whatever she did, Ainsley knew she couldn't fall asleep—no matter how much her body demanded it.

She tried to move again, to get out of her binds.

But it was no use.

She'd have to wait until the sedative wore off.

But she had no idea how long that would take, considering the drug-drenched cloths were all still pressed against her skin.

"I NEED to see security footage from these hallways," Carter said.

Greta nodded nervously as they stood outside Ainsley's empty treatment room. "Of course. But we'll have to go down to the security desk to—"

Carter locked his gaze with hers. "You have cameras behind your desk. I saw them."

Her hand fluttered through the air as she tried to explain. "Yes, but I can get in trouble if I—"

"Do I have to go over this with you again? My wife could be in danger. I need to know what's happening with her. Now."

Just then, Hayes burst into the spa.

Carter knew they weren't supposed to associate with each other. But how could they not?

The only thing that made Carter feel better was the fact no one else was in the lobby.

"Is this . . . your backup or something?" Greta stammered as she looked at Hayes.

"Something like that. He's going to help me find Ainsley. Now can you pull up that footage?"

She glanced at them again before nodding. Carter and Hayes followed her to the other side of the desk and watched as she scrolled through the recording.

Carter's breath caught when he saw a man carrying Ainsley from her room.

His shoulders tightened as he pointed to the image. "Who is that?"

"I've . . . I don't know. I've never seen him before," Greta stuttered. "I mean it. I haven't."

"Keep following him on the camera." Hayes bristled as he stepped closer.

Greta hit a few more buttons, and the camera switched angles.

They watched as the man slipped out another door at the end of the hallway.

"Where does that hallway lead?" Hayes asked.

"To a service corridor that connects each of the shops and businesses for employees."

"So, from that hallway, this guy could basically go anywhere," Carter clarified.

"I . . . I guess. I mean . . . I think I'm going to need to call security." Greta frowned nervously.

"I think you're going to need to do that," Carter said. "In the meantime, my friend and I are going to look for her. You're not going to try to stop us."

"Of course not."

Without saying anything else, Carter and Hayes took off.

———

She just had to move.

That's what Ainsley kept telling herself.

The more she moved, the looser the cloths around her would become.

The less effect these drugs would have on her.

That would all be easier if her head wasn't swimming and nausea wasn't swirling in her gut.

Why had someone done this to her?

The question kept repeating in her mind.

But right now, she simply needed to focus on survival.

Move, Ainsley. Move. Your life might depend on it.

She tried to wiggle some more, but whoever had wrapped her up had done a good job. She was trapped.

Finally, she rested her head on the cool tile

beneath her and tried to inhale a few deep breaths. Maybe the drugs were wearing off just a little.

How long would it be before anyone noticed that she was missing?

Carter was hanging out with the guys in the steam room. Who knew how long they'd be gone?

Hayes was tailing Carter, so her colleague wouldn't know anything was wrong.

Even if Charlie tried to check in, Ainsley didn't have her phone with her.

This whole thing felt like a no-win situation.

By the time anyone figured out Ainsley was missing, that guy could return and take her somewhere else.

She may not ever be seen again.

Flashbacks hit her.

Flashbacks of when Dante had cornered her in Austin.

Flashbacks of hearing him breathe in her ear.

Of feeling his fingers squeezing her neck.

Of seeing the evil in his eyes.

He'd locked her in his root cellar, and Ainsley had been certain she would die there.

But she hadn't.

She'd managed to escape.

Managed to track down Dante.

He'd been arrested, and her nightmare had been over.

So she'd thought.

If not Dante, who was after her now?

She pressed her eyes closed and began praying.

Because at this point, that was all she could do.

CHAPTER
THIRTY

CARTER AND HAYES reached the employee hallway and paused.

Hayes turned to him. "You go right. I'll go left."

Wasting no more time, Carter took off.

He would search each doorway if he had to. Question everyone he ran into.

Whatever it took to find Ainsley.

Had she been taken because of him?

Carter would have to sort through those details later.

Right now, he just needed to find her.

He didn't even care if he broke cover.

That suddenly wasn't important anymore.

He opened the first doorway, but it was only an office.

A woman stared at him, lowering her reading glasses before asking, "Can I help you?"

Carter quickly shut the door and moved to the next.

A storage closet. But no Ainsley.

Carter searched more rooms—another office, more closets, some back entries to a game room, a café, and the gift shop. If he saw anyone inside, he asked them if they'd seen a woman come through.

No one had. There was no Ainsley.

Carter froze when he spotted a figure at the end of the hallway.

It was the man from the security footage—the one who'd been carrying Ainsley.

"Hey!" Carter shouted.

The man's eyes lit with alarm.

Then he took off in a run in the opposite direction.

Carter took off after him, but then stopped.

The man had been going to get Ainsley, hadn't he?

That meant that Ainsley might be in one of the rooms on this hallway.

He grabbed his phone and quickly called Hayes, giving him the update. Maybe Hayes could catch this guy.

It didn't even matter right now.

All that mattered was finding Ainsley.

Carter opened the nearest door and saw a closet full of towels.

He almost closed it.

Then he saw something out of place in the corner.

A pile of blankets on the floor.

No. Not just blankets.

Someone was wrapped in the blankets.

Lying there unmoving.

Ainsley . . .

The breath left his lungs.

Was she even still alive?

———

Ainsley felt warm water hitting her.

She was in the shower, she thought. Two people stood over her, talking in muted tones.

Then there were more voices. Someone sounded as if he were giving instructions.

Urgency stretched through the air.

Ainsley wasn't in that closet anymore.

Someone had carried her somewhere.

Everything was still blurred around her.

But she could move.

The blanket was gone.

She blinked several times.

What was happening?

Carter had rescued her, hadn't he?

Even though everything was blurry, she recognized his voice.

She tried to say something, but only a moan escaped. Would the water wash away the effects of these drugs? They were already in her system.

What had they wrapped her in? Was this just a temporary effect? What if it was something more lethal?

Her heart pounded as if it might jump out of her chest.

"It's going to be okay," a deep voice said.

Carter.

She thought he was gripping her hand.

A moment later, everything went black again.

CHAPTER
THIRTY-ONE

CARTER STAYED by Ainsley's side as she lay in a bed in a small clinic at the resort. They had a doctor on standby, and he'd given Ainsley a shot to reverse the effects of the sedatives in her body.

Hayes had disappeared before anyone spotted him. However, if Jack looked at the security camera footage, he'd see Hayes.

Carter wasn't sure how he'd explain the man's presence—unless he said Hayes was a stranger who'd stepped in to help. That seemed like the best excuse.

Carter continued to hold Ainsley's hand as he waited.

As a shadow appeared in the doorway, he looked behind him.

Jack.

"I heard what happened." He stepped inside and shook his head, a grim look on his face. "I can't believe it."

Carter squeezed Ainsley's hand, his chest tightening with apprehension. "Me neither."

"I'm having my people look into it. Whoever that guy was, he doesn't work for me."

"Why would someone attack Ainsley?" Carter really wanted to know the answer to that question. He also needed to remember to stay in character. He thought the inquiry was safe enough.

"I have no idea." Jack rubbed his jaw and frowned. "Unless it's because of you and me. There are many people who want to bring me down. There are other people who realize what a great and powerful team we would make. Maybe someone knows that, and they want to stop it before anything could happen."

Carter's eyebrows flickered up. "Do you think somebody would do that?"

Jack's gaze met his. "You'd be amazed at some of the things people do for money and power. I'm only sorry that Ainsley may have taken the brunt of some of that. What did the doctor say?"

Carter glanced back down at Ainsley as she let out a soft moan. "They're doing testing on those cloths to see what was put on them."

"I talked to her technician myself. Someone else put the cloths for the wrap in the warmer for her, so she never touched them beforehand. This guy must have known what was happening and substituted the cloths they usually use for these drug-laced ones."

Carter didn't like the sound of that. "This would've taken some planning. Should we call the police?"

Jack twisted his head. "If that makes you more comfortable, we can. But I personally like handling things myself."

"I understand that." Carter shifted. "But I can't stop thinking about this. Who knew she was going to the spa today?"

Jack shrugged. "Just my team and I, I suppose. I'll talk to Eric and see if he told anybody else. I don't know what's going on here, but I promise you that I will do everything to find some answers."

That was a two-edged sword, Carter realized.

Yes, he did want some answers. But if Jack dug too deeply, he might discover the truth about Carter and Ainsley. He couldn't let that happen either.

He would need to figure out a way out of this.

But right now, his only concern was Ainsley.

Ainsley pulled her eyes open, her mind still groggy. She blinked several times as a face in front of her came into view.

Carter.

"You're awake," he murmured. "I'm so glad."

He sounded so concerned. So sincere.

Ainsley had to remind herself that he didn't really care about her. That he didn't trust her. That this was all an act.

She glanced around.

No one else was in the room with them right now.

She tried to push herself up, her head throbbing. "What happened?"

Carter explained about her being drugged, abducted, and then rescued. He ended by telling her that she was being treated at the clinic at the lodge.

She raked a hand through her hair. "I can't believe this."

"I wasn't expecting anything like this to happen either. I'm glad that I found you when I did. I don't know what that guy was planning to do with you, and I don't even want to think about it." His voice cracked.

She glanced at Carter and saw that vein protruding in his temple. Saw how his nostrils flared.

He wasn't faking this.

He really had been concerned, hadn't he?

She wanted to say things to him. But she didn't dare. Not here. For all she knew Jack could have some type of listening device in here. They couldn't risk that.

"Thank you for finding me," she said instead.

"Always." His gaze caught hers.

Always? What did that even mean?

Certainly, Carter was just playing it up. He had to realize there could be listening devices in here.

Whatever Ainsley did, she couldn't take his words to heart.

"Do they know what was given to me?" she asked.

"They think it was some type of transdermal opioid." He shrugged. "They'll have to send those cloths off to be tested, of course."

"I want to go back to our room." Her voice came out as a whisper.

Carter offered a definitive head shake. "I'm not sure that's a good idea."

"What time is it? How long have I been out?" Nothing was making sense to her. She hated feeling so disoriented, so . . . weak.

"I found you about an hour ago."

An hour . . . she slowly processed that. "So we haven't missed dinner yet?"

Carter frowned. "In light of everything that's happened—"

"We should still go," she quickly interjected. "We didn't come all the way here so I could lie in bed and rest."

"But—"

Her gaze locked with his. "I'll be fine. I just need my clothes and my purse, and I would like to go back to our suite."

As Carter looked at her, Ainsley waited for him to argue with her more.

But this was one argument he wouldn't win.

CHAPTER
THIRTY-TWO

CARTER STILL FELT UNEASY. He really wanted to take Ainsley far away from The Everly.

In fact, he wished she'd never gotten wrapped up in this whole situation at all. He should have come alone. That had been his first instinct, and he should have listened to it.

However, now Ainsley was here. Maybe he could send her home. Say she wasn't feeling well and needed to leave. But he could stay here to find that information. Maybe Hayes could even stay here with him to keep an eye on things.

To Carter that sounded like a better idea.

But he knew Ainsley would never go for it.

Besides, the way people were talking, the roads to this area might close soon. Snowplows were having trouble keeping them clear.

The doctor cleared Ainsley to go if she felt up to walking.

Eric had brought a bag full of clothes from the gift shop as well as the clothes she'd worn to the spa and her purse, and then shut the door so she could change.

She gave Carter a pointed look first. "Turn around."

Ordinarily, he'd leave the room. But they were supposed to be married, so that would raise too many questions. Jack or any of his associates could return at any moment. They couldn't take that chance.

Instead, he didn't even argue. He just turned, giving her the privacy that she needed.

"I'm done," she said after a few moments.

He glanced back at her and saw the black joggers and T-shirt with *The Everly* written across them. Her hair was pulled back into a bun, and she'd probably want to take a shower.

Otherwise, she looked fine. Maybe a little worse for the wear, but not that bad, all things considered.

She took a step forward and nearly stumbled.

Carter rushed toward her and took her arm. He expected her to shrug him off, but she didn't.

"Let's get you back to the room," he muttered.

For the first time, she didn't argue.

Ainsley knew she had to pull herself together. But if she were to be truthful, she was shaken by what had happened. She stayed on guard, looking out for a lot of things. Gunmen. Stalkers. Drug runners.

But she'd never expected this.

Even more unnerving was the fact that Ainsley wasn't sure if this had something to do with her stalker or with Jack Earl.

As soon as she and Carter reached their room and the door was locked behind them, she finally felt like she could breathe.

The big soirée this evening was in three hours.

That meant Ainsley had three hours to pull herself together.

She hoped that wouldn't be a problem.

"Are you sure you're okay?" Carter lingered close as if afraid she might fall.

Ainsley nodded and pushed herself away from the wall. She hadn't even realized she was leaning against it, breathing entirely too heavily.

She couldn't let Carter know how shaken she was. She didn't want him to lose confidence in her abilities. She was supposed to be watching out for him, after all.

"I just need to give Charlie a call and give her an update on what's going on," she finally said.

Carter studied her a moment. "Of course."

But as Ainsley walked to the couch and lowered herself there, she noticed Carter still watching her, still lingering close as if she were fragile.

She dug through her purse.

Her heart nearly stopped.

Her gun.

It was gone.

Who had taken it?

And what were they planning on doing with it?

Her heart kicked into overdrive.

Quickly, she found her phone and called Charlie.

Charlie answered on the first ring, and Ainsley gave her the update.

"I don't like this." Charlie's voice sounded grim.

"Believe me—neither do I." Ainsley pulled her knees to her chest. "I should've been more alert."

"You couldn't have known."

Charlie's words made her feel better, but Ainsley still knew the truth. She shouldn't have let down her guard.

"I'm tempted to bring you back," Charlie said.

"I don't like quitting."

Ainsley meant the words. Quitting wasn't in her vocabulary.

Charlie remained quiet a moment before finally letting out a soft grunt. "Okay. But if anything else happens, I'm pulling you out. I can't put you at risk."

"If I was a male, you wouldn't be saying I should come home now."

Charlie sighed. "You've got me there. Although there have been many times, I've wanted to pull my guys from their assignments. But I'm not trying to handle you with kid gloves. I promise you that. I know you're very capable."

"Thank you." Ainsley felt a little better at Charlie's words.

"I do have an update on the detonator."

Any of the relief Ainsley felt disappeared faster than snow in the sun. "What's that?"

"The one in your purse . . . we believe it may be connected with the bomb in Maureen's car. It's hard to know for sure since the bomb destroyed much of the evidence. But the basics match."

Dread pooled in her stomach.

That wasn't what Ainsley wanted to hear.

"In the meantime, what's next for you?" Charlie asked.

"There's a big, fancy get-together tonight in Jack Earl's suite. Since that's where he's staying, we're thinking that's where that hard drive might be. We're trying to formulate a plan on how to get our hands on it."

"He's smart. He's not going to make it easy."

"I know." Ainsley frowned at the thought. "And that's what worries me."

THIRTY-THREE

CARTER DIDN'T WANT Ainsley to go to the party tonight.

He knew he had some trust issues with her. He knew he'd doubted her.

But another part of him knew he still cared about her.

That he'd always cared about her.

Now he had to figure out what to do about it.

For everything there is a season, a time for every activity under heaven. He'd just read that this morning during his Bible study time.

What purpose could the events of this weekend have?

"Why are you looking at me like that?" Ainsley stared at him as they sat on the couch beside each other.

Carter almost dismissed her question. Then he decided not to.

"I need you to answer some questions for me."

Her eyebrows rose in curiosity. "Like what?"

"How did that detonator get in your purse?"

Ainsley let out a long, heavy breath. "I have no way of proving this, but someone planted it there. That's why they sent you that text. This person wanted you to find it and to doubt me."

The more he thought about it, the more that made sense. The person who'd sent that text hadn't done so to warn him. They wanted to play with his head.

For a while, it had worked.

"One more question: what happened with this Dante guy?" Carter leaned toward her as he waited for her answer.

Her eyebrows shot up before she tugged the blanket around her. "Why are you asking about him?"

"Because what happened to you today could have been because of Jack. Or it could be Dante or someone working with Dante. I need to know more. My safety is on the line right now also." Carter wasn't worried about his own safety, but he thought that argument might have merit with her.

Ainsley let out another sigh and glanced at the clock.

They had enough time before tonight's social to have this conversation. Carter felt confident of it.

"While I was on patrol as a Texas Ranger, I stopped to help someone whose car had broken down in the middle of nowhere," she finally started. "It was a man in his thirties, and he knew nothing about cars. I was able to fix it for him—I just had to jiggle a few wires—and I sent him on his way. I thought that was it. No big deal, right?"

Carter could see fear glaze Ainsley's eyes as her mind reeled back in time.

"A few days later, this guy showed up at my Ranger station, and he brought me flowers to say thank you. I found out his name was Dante. The guys thought it was cute and gave me a hard time about it. I thanked him, but I was careful not to give him any of the wrong signals. I could see something off in his gaze. He was socially awkward, to say the least."

Carter had a feeling he knew where this was going, but he waited.

Ainsley rubbed her thumb over her fingers before continuing. "Dante showed up at my house one day after work. He brought a yellow rose with him. I had to get blunt with him. I had to tell him that he couldn't keep approaching me. That I wasn't interested. That I'd just simply been doing my job. But he didn't get it. I could tell that by the look in his eyes."

"What happened next?"

"It just kept progressing. The friendly, clueless guy disappeared. The more I rejected him, the more hardened he became. He broke into my house. I had to get a restraining order against him. He transformed into a different person. Turns out he had a history of domestic violence."

Carter grunted.

"My captain finally told me to take a week and get away. My colleagues were going to try to arrest him on another charge and put him behind bars. So I went to my friend's cabin. I was sure no one else followed me there. But that night, I woke up, and he was in my room—standing over my bed, staring at me as I slept."

Before Carter realized what he was doing, he reached forward and grabbed her hand.

Ainsley froze for a moment, looking uncertain how to respond.

But she didn't pull away.

"He injected me with something. When I woke up again, I was in a root cellar. He kept me there for two days before I managed to get away. I kept thinking about my training as a Ranger. So I stayed calm. When I saw the first opportunity, I hit Dante over the head with an old glass jar I'd found half buried in the dirt. I locked him in the cellar and ran until I could flag down a car and use their phone. He was arrested."

Carter couldn't help but think how things might have turned out differently if he'd been in her life.

But he hadn't been. He'd made mistakes. She'd pushed him out.

They'd both grown and changed.

Yet they were here now.

How could he change things for their future?

———

Ainsley stared at Carter's hand as it gripped hers.

She wanted to believe the motion was because he cared about her.

But she couldn't let herself go there. Last time she had, he'd broken her heart. She couldn't put herself through that again.

Instead, she pulled her hand back into her lap.

She didn't know how she felt after sharing that. She never talked about Dante. But she felt as if she owed Carter an explanation.

However, seeing the compassion in his gaze mixed with uncertainty nearly left her undone.

She had to get herself together.

She cleared her throat as she looked up at him. "Now is it my turn?"

He tilted his head. "You want to ask me a question?"

Ainsley nodded. "I do."

He paused a moment before he shrugged. "Okay. Go for it."

She shifted on the couch. "Why were you meeting with Maureen? What kind of deal were you finalizing?"

Surprise flickered through his gaze. "That? It was nothing."

"If it was nothing, then tell me what it was."

"You think I was doing some backhanded deal or something?"

Ainsley didn't say anything.

Carter let out a breath, clearly uncomfortable with her question. "If you really want to know . . . I was setting up a charitable trust that will funnel money from my investments into charities of my choice."

She flinched. "What?"

Carter nodded. "It sounds prideful if I tell people, and that's not what I want. I don't want attention for what I'm doing."

"You're giving away all your money?" Had she heard him correctly?

"I'm keeping enough to live on. The truth is, I make a lot of money on the technology I developed. More than I deserve. More than I could ever use. I've seen how money can destroy people, and that's not what I want for my life. So I decided to set up a trust and funnel that money to them so the funds can go for a good cause—to people who need it."

That was the last thing Ainsley had expected to hear.

She still didn't know what to think of it.

Was it possible that she'd been wrong about Carter?

She didn't know.

But the thought of it left her feeling off-balance.

And she didn't like feeling off-balance.

Instead, she rushed to her feet, suddenly needing some time alone so she could clear her head. "I should start getting ready."

Carter stared at her a moment before nodding. "Of course."

But really, she was just anxious to get away.

CHAPTER
THIRTY-FOUR

AS CARTER STRAIGHTENED HIS TIE, he looked in the mirror again, and his thoughts wandered to Ainsley as she got ready in the bathroom.

He was worried about her. It wasn't that she wasn't tough and capable. She could clearly take care of herself.

But whoever was behind these incidents, whether it be her stalker or someone connected with Jack Earl, was clever.

He and Ainsley would need to watch their every step.

As the door opened, he turned his head.

Ainsley stepped from the bathroom, and Carter instantly felt his throat go dry.

She was a total knockout.

Even though she was of medium height, her high heels made her seem much taller. Her honey-blonde hair had been twisted back. She had put on entirely more makeup than usual, and her dress wasn't the standard black.

Instead, she'd chosen a simple royal-blue dress that stretched to her knees and fit her like a glove, as the saying went.

Before Carter realized what he was doing, he let out a low whistle. "You look great."

"Thanks." But Ainsley didn't sound happy as she said the words.

If Carter knew her like he thought he did, she'd much rather be in jeans and cowboy boots right now.

But she could clearly pull off both looks.

Glancing at her now, one couldn't even tell anything about her earlier ordeal. Her eyes looked bright and her movements fluid.

As she stepped closer, she let out a long sigh, almost as if exhausted. "You ready to go?"

He studied her face another moment. "Are you sure you're up for this?"

"This is what I came here for."

For some reason, Ainsley's words caused Carter's chest to deflate just a little bit. Maybe part of him had hoped she'd taken this assignment for him.

Of course, he knew that wasn't true.

Yet he'd be in denial if he said he didn't still have feelings for her.

Hardly a week went by that Carter didn't think about Ainsley. About what might have been if only things had turned out differently. Sure, he'd dated other women since Ainsley.

But no one had ever measured up, had made him feel that same zing.

"We better get going or we'll be late." Ainsley grabbed a small black clutch and placed it under her arm.

Her voice pulled Carter from his thoughts.

As he stepped out into the hallway—first, checking it to make sure the coast was clear—Ainsley looped her arm through his, and they started toward Jack's suite, located the next floor up.

"We have a plan?" Carter waited until they were on the elevator alone to ask the question.

He knew they'd talked about this, but it just felt like he needed more certainty.

"Unfortunately, we're going to need to play this by ear. We haven't seen the inside of Jack's place, and we don't know exactly what Jack brought with him. You don't worry about anything. I'll do the dirty work while you mingle."

Carter didn't like the sound of that.

Just what was Ainsley thinking? And how much danger would it put her in?

———

Ainsley plastered on a smile as she stepped inside Jack's suite.

He'd greeted them at the door, looking like a movie star in his designer suit and shoes. His wavy hair was slicked back from his face, and he was freshly shaven.

Haley looked just as Ainsley had expected—gorgeous in a slinky white sequined dress and high heels.

An air of haughtiness filled the entire room.

Ainsley couldn't wait to have this over with.

These kinds of people just weren't her kind of people.

She preferred to be around people who didn't mind hard work or physical labor. Who would drop anything and everything if a friend needed them. Who knew the importance of balance—of hard work combined with kicking back with family and friends.

Basically, she preferred salt of the earth people.

The air of superficiality around this crowd made her uncomfortable.

"Are you feeling better?" Jack asked as he led her from the doorway into a living area.

Ainsley nearly forgot his question when she looked out the windows.

She'd seen this view earlier, she supposed, but the vista seemed even more striking right now.

Two stories of windows. She knew the mountains were in the background, but it was dark outside now. However, the ski slopes were lit and the chairlifts were running. The window showcased skiers as they wove their way down the thick, fluffy snow.

"Do you like it?" Jack appeared beside her.

She smiled as she glanced at him. "It's stunning."

"Now you can see why I wanted to buy this place."

"Yes, I can."

He pointed to a lift to the west. "That's my own personal ski lift. It takes me to my private ski chalet. It's one of the perks of owning this place."

Ainsley's eyebrows shot up. "I'd say."

Jack shifted. "Now, about my earlier question, Ainsley. How are you feeling after your ordeal today?"

"I'm much better now. Thank you. Any updates on the person who did this to me? As you can imagine, I'm quite concerned."

Carter appeared beside her, his hand slipping

around her waist, as if it was what he always did. Something about the action felt a little too natural.

"I have my security team here working on it, but we believe someone snuck into our facilities to do this," Jack said. "Clearly, it was someone with an inside connection since he knew you'd be at the spa and which room you were in. But they could've accessed the computer to figure that out."

"Did you talk to the woman who did the wrap treatment on Ainsley?"

"We're trying to find her now."

"What about the other receptionist?" Carter asked. "Kathy, I think. Were you able to talk to her?"

"Apparently, all of this happened during a switch in the shifts. She didn't see anyone, but she's terribly shaken up about it. I assure you, we're working hard to figure this out."

"I appreciate that," Ainsley said. "I'll sleep better once I know this guy is in police custody."

"You and me both."

As Jack said the words, her gaze traveled to the rest of the room and stopped at a table.

A table where a dozen yellow roses rested in a crystal vase.

She reeled at the sight.

CHAPTER
THIRTY-FIVE

CARTER FOLLOWED Ainsley's gaze and saw the roses.

His chest squeezed with apprehension.

"Thanks for the roses." Jack turned back to them. "It was nice of you to send those. But unnecessary. It's my pleasure to have you both here."

Carter blinked, unsure if he'd understood what Jack said.

Jack thought Carter and Ainsley had sent those roses?

He stared at the flowers. Was there a card with them? Had someone tried to send another message?

Later, maybe he'd try to get closer. To take a better look.

"Yellow roses are beautiful, aren't they?" Thankfully, Ainsley jumped in.

"I think so too." Jack turned to the rest of the crowd.

The group mingled with drinks in their hands. Apparently, several other people had been invited to this event also, other board members at NorthStar.

Carter hadn't thought that so many people were going to be here. Maybe that could work to their advantage.

"I invited some members of the board," Jack explained as if reading his thoughts. "I thought it would be nice if you got a feel for our whole organization."

Part of Carter was annoyed at Jack's assumptions. But another part of him thought that maybe this could be a good thing. Maybe somebody else here knew something.

"Can we get a tour of this place?" Ainsley asked.

"Of course."

Jack led them around the deluxe space.

He showed off his living room and kitchen, three bedrooms, a small soaking pool, and hot tub, three bathrooms, and uncountable closets. Jack apparently had an affinity for saltwater aquariums also. There were several in the space, each immaculate. Jack explained they were a hobby of his.

Carter had no doubt Ainsley had asked for a tour because she wanted to locate Jack's hard drive, not because she was curious about this man's extravagant lifestyle.

As they stepped away from the crowd and into a hallway, Jack turned to them, pressing his lips together, as if he was about to say something important.

"Since I have both of you alone for a moment, there's something I wanted to ask you," he started. "What exactly is going on between the two of you? Don't tell me nothing because I know that's not true."

Ainsley felt her breath catch as she swallowed hard.

Did Jack know her marriage to Carter was fake?

Had he checked into their marriage license?

Brody, Vanishing Ranch's computer guy, had sorted all that out. He was the best at what he did. So that shouldn't be a problem.

"I just feel as if you've been jumpy," Jack said. "Like there's more to this story. Then after what happened today . . ."

Ainsley glanced at Carter, exchanging a silent conversation.

Then Ainsley took Carter's hand into hers and squeezed it as she moved closer. "I didn't want to say anything, but someone has been stalking me. I'm afraid he's here now."

Jack's eyebrows shot up. "What?"

She nodded, not having to fake the terror in her gaze. "Several things happened before I left home, but I hoped they were my imagination. Since I've been here, I've felt like someone's been watching me. I think it might be him. So I apologize if I seem jumpy. But the situation has me on edge."

"Don't apologize. That's good to know." Jack's eyes narrowed. "I realize you probably didn't want to tell me that but, now that I know, I'll make sure my security guards have someone keep an eye out for him."

"I appreciate that. Thank you." She offered a brief description of the man.

"Okay, enough of this heavy conversation." Jack rolled his shoulders back and released a pent-up breath. "Now, I have a lot of people I need to introduce you to."

Ainsley felt relief rush through her.

Maybe she'd thrown Jack's suspicions off her for now.

But she dreaded all the schmoozing she would have to do next in order to stay in character.

CARTER WAS SMILING SO MUCH that his jaw literally hurt.

They were already more than an hour into this event, and all he wanted to do was go back to his suite.

Most people didn't believe him when he said he was a homebody.

But he was.

He preferred a small close-knit group of people and low-key outings to this kind of extravagance.

The good news was that he'd been able to wander closer to the roses.

There had been a card.

A typed note had read: "The best is yet to come."

Carter knew exactly what that meant. This situation was going to get worse before it got better.

Dread thrummed in his nerves as he anticipated what might transpire.

Across the room, he saw Ainsley talking to Haley and Brooke and wandered their way.

He'd tried not to let her out of his sight for the entire party. Even though it seemed as if this would be a safe space, he'd quickly learned that nowhere was really safe.

He walked up just in time to hear Ainsley say, "Which one of you was the one who recommended that weight loss wrap?"

Brooke's hand flew over her mouth. "It was me. Of course, I had no idea that this would happen. I get those done at least once a month . . . I mean, who would've thought?"

Something about the way the woman said the words didn't strike Carter as sincere.

Maybe Brooke truly did feel bad about it, but he didn't trust the woman yet.

He didn't trust Haley yet either.

For that matter, maybe he shouldn't trust Ainsley.

But being a lone ranger certainly was exhausting. It would be nice to have at least one person he could truly trust and depend on. He wasn't sure he'd ever have that, though.

When he'd first started in the tech business, he'd had a partner. The guy had taken one of Carter's ideas and claimed it as his own. Worse yet, he'd thought the man was his friend.

That experience had shifted the way he viewed others in this business.

"If you'll excuse me," Ainsley started. "I really need to run to the restroom."

"It's just right down that hallway." Haley nodded toward the space.

"I'll find it." Ainsley gave Carter a lingering look before she headed that way.

One that said she was clearly up to something.

Dread pooled in his stomach as he wondered what that might be.

———

Ainsley took one more glance behind her before she stepped down the hallway.

But she didn't have to go to the bathroom.

Instead, she slipped into Jack Earl's room and quietly closed the door behind her.

Quickly, Ainsley surveyed the space. But she knew she was alone.

She'd been keeping tabs on people all night, and she knew where everyone was.

She sucked in a deep breath before pushing herself from the door.

Jack had a small desk set up in the corner with his computer.

This guy was too smart to keep anything there. Charlie had said much of the information Jack had on people was kept on some type of hard drive—probably one that had been disguised.

Part of Ainsley thought that he was too smart to bring this device with him.

But it was also risky to leave it behind, even in a safety deposit box. Jack probably even had more than one copy if she read the man correctly.

He was smart enough that he couldn't risk something happening to this asset.

Quickly, Ainsley began searching the room, looking for anything that could be this storage device.

Would Jack have put it in the safe?

It was a decent guess, especially since he owned this place.

She opened the closet door and saw the safe there.

In just a few minutes, she should be able to access this.

Working quickly, she pulled a device from her purse and hooked it up to the keypad there. She'd snagged a glass Jack had been drinking out of earlier, and she'd pretended it was her own.

Now that she was out of sight, she took some

powder and putty from her purse and extracted one of his prints from the glass.

It felt very OO-7ish.

But the method worked.

A moment later, she pressed the print into the biometric lock.

Just as the device clicked, she heard the door to the room open.

She froze.

Someone else was coming.

Ainsley shut the closet door before tucking herself in the closet corner.

She prayed no one found her.

AINSLEY HAD BEEN GONE for too long.

And Carter was worried.

He knew she hadn't gone to the bathroom.

He'd double-checked the room just in case.

Ainsley hadn't been there.

Then he'd wandered farther down the hallway.

That's when the realization hit him.

She'd gone into Jack's room, hadn't she?

His breath caught. She should have told him. Should have let him go along.

But Carter knew that may not have been smart either. With both Ainsley and Carter gone, someone would be more likely to notice.

Still, he could have at least been on guard for her.

He glanced around to make sure no one was looking.

Then he slipped into Jack's bedroom.

Darkness surrounded him.

It took a moment for his eyes to adjust.

Nothing inside looked touched.

He didn't see Ainsley either.

Where was she? What if someone had grabbed her again?

The questions—and concerns—raced through his head.

He'd quickly search the room to make sure Ainsley wasn't here. Then he'd figure out a Plan B.

He walked around the bed. No Ainsley.

Into the bathroom. Ainsley wasn't there either.

There weren't that many places in this room where she could hide.

He paused by the closet.

But just as he started to open the door, something shuffled inside, and he froze.

***

Ainsley peered through the small crack between the door and the wall.

She sucked in a breath.

Was that . . . Carter?

She slowly released the air from her lungs.

Wasting no more time, she pushed open the door and stared at him. "What are you doing in here?"

"Ainsley?" He let out a breath and then ran a hand through his hair. "I thought something had happened to you."

"I told you I was coming here to get information," she whispered, a fussy edge to her voice.

"I'm sorry. But I was worried. Especially after everything that's happened."

Her shoulders softened. "I appreciate that, but we're more at risk if we're both gone."

He raised his hands in surrender. "Sorry . . ."

"Since you're already here, go to the door and keep watch for me. If you hear anyone coming down the hallway, let me know."

"Will do." He walked back that way.

As he did, she opened the lock.

A small, external hard drive waited there.

A sense of victory surged through Ainsley.

Her celebration didn't last long, however.

That was too easy.

Jack was too smart to leave a hard drive in a safe, even with the biometric lock.

What was she missing?

If she were Jack Earl, how would she disguise this hard drive so no one would find it, but so that she could also take it wherever she went.

She stared at the safe, wondering what she was missing.

An idea hit her.

Was she crazy?

Maybe.

But maybe not.

She ran her hands along the small safe—one that wasn't attached to the wall.

She would think that Jack would have something more heavy duty. Something more permanent. But it almost looked as if he'd brought this safe with him.

Which seemed strange.

Her fingers stopped at something at the back of the metal box.

Her breath caught.

It was a USB port.

This safe was the hard drive, she realized.

The device inside was just a decoy to distract anyone who might come looking.

Ainsley pulled an external hard drive from her purse.

Quickly, she plugged it into the USB on the safe.

A little timer indicated the download would take five minutes.

Five minutes? Did they have that long?

She frowned. Ainsley had really been hoping that this might get them somewhere.

She didn't know how many other opportunities she'd have to get in here and find out this information.

The minutes seemed to drag by.

"What's taking so long?" Carter asked. "Someone's going to look for us."

"I know! Just thirty more seconds."

Finally, the device dinged.

Relief filled her.

Quickly, she put the device back into her purse and closed the safe. Then she stepped from the closet and closed the door, leaving the space just as she had found it.

As she headed toward the door, Carter said, "Someone's coming. What are we going to do?"

THIRTY-EIGHT

AINSLEY KNEW she needed to think quickly.

What possible reason could they have for being in here?

She strode across the room until she reached Carter.

Right before the door opened, she pushed him against the wall and pressed her lips into his.

He stiffened, but only for a moment before he seemed to realize what she was doing.

Then his hands circled her waist, and he drew her closer.

Ainsley wrapped her arms around his neck as their kiss deepened. As her fingers played with the hair at the nape of his neck. As she relished in the scent of his spicy aftershave.

It was all an act.

Still, they needed to make it believable.

Ainsley didn't think that would be a problem.

She was quickly becoming lost in the kiss.

So lost that she barely heard the door open.

A shadow covered them, and then someone said, "Oh sorry . . . I didn't know you two were in here."

Eric had found them.

Ainsley pulled back just slightly, but still kept an arm wrapped around Carter's neck. She quickly wiped her lips and looked away as if embarrassed.

"Sorry," Carter started. "We just got married last week, and . . ."

Eric raised a hand. "You don't have to explain. But you can't be in here."

Carter pushed himself off the wall and loosened his arms from around Ainsley. Instead, he took her hand and said, "Sorry again. We got a little carried away."

Eric grunted. "It happens."

As Eric started to leave, Ainsley called to him, and he paused.

"Is there any way we could keep this between us? I mean, I'd hate for something like this to ruin Carter's chances of being hired . . ." She offered a pouty frown.

"Understood." Eric's gaze remained on them a moment longer as they all stepped from the room.

Ainsley thought he'd bought their excuse. Or he could be a great actor.

He could be the true mastermind here.

But her pulse still pounded out of control as she realized just how amazing that staged kiss had been.

———

Carter couldn't stop thinking about that kiss.

Couldn't stop thinking about how he wanted to do it again. And again. And again.

It reminded him of the kiss he and Ainsley had shared all those years ago. The one he'd never forgotten.

Probably because he'd never experienced so much chemistry and connection like he had with Ainsley.

His lips still tingled, and his heart still pounded at the memory.

As they joined the rest of the crowd, Ainsley leaned closer. "Sorry I pounced on you."

"No apologies necessary."

She gave him a questioning look—so questioning it was almost flirtatious.

But Carter wasn't going to assume too much.

"Do you think we got what we needed?" he whispered.

Ainsley glanced around before nodding. "I think so."

A sense of victory surged through him.

That situation had been a close call.

If Jack had caught them in his room and knew what they were really up to . . . their lives would be in even greater danger.

But it was more than that. Carter needed to figure out what had really happened to his father. So far, he was getting nowhere.

The stakes were climbing, and he was running out of time to get the information he needed.

But for now, he and Ainsley had to make it through the rest of this social.

CHAPTER
THIRTY-NINE

AINSLEY'S ADRENALINE was still pumping when they finally left the party two hours later.

She and Carter had acted lovey-dovey, like the perfect newlyweds, as they held hands and laughed at each other's jokes.

But as they walked out, she realized they were still holding hands.

"You know we don't have to hold hands anymore," she murmured.

"What if I just want to?" Carter raised an eyebrow.

She started to reprimand him, but then she realized that someone could still be watching. Maybe it was a good idea if they continued to hold hands. It was the only reason she didn't let go.

At least, that's what Ainsley told herself.

As they climbed into the elevator, and they were alone again, her thoughts went back to that kiss.

Part of her would like nothing more than to wrap herself in his arms again and to pick up exactly where they left off.

She scolded herself. She couldn't think like that. She'd come here to do a job, not to rekindle a relationship with the man who had broken her heart.

As Carter stepped closer in the elevator, her pulse began throbbing again.

Oh no . . . this was bad.

In fact, Ainsley was close enough to him that all she needed to do was look up, lean forward, and . . .

"What do you think we'll find?" he asked.

Carter's question startled her from her thoughts, and she took a slight step back, hoping he didn't see the desire in her eyes.

"I don't know, but we'll know soon enough." She opened her purse and showed him the drive. "This could be exactly what we're looking for."

Carter stared at the device as if it were a trophy. "If there's something there, I'll figure out what it is."

"I know you will." Was that a slight tinge of pride in her voice?

Ainsley would need to watch herself.

Thankfully, the elevator dinged just then, and they headed to their suite.

But as soon as they stepped inside, Ainsley knew something was wrong.

Someone else had been there.

———

"Ainsley?" Carter stared at the room, sensing something was off.

"Stay here," Ainsley muttered.

Carter wanted to argue, but he knew better than to do that.

Still, tension filled his body as he anticipated what Ainsley might find.

Whoever was after them wasn't giving up. They weren't shy about letting them know that danger was near, either.

Ainsley searched the room, the bathroom, and the closet before coming back. She'd even checked under the beds.

Carter started to say something when she shook her head and put her finger over her mouth.

Then she went to one of the bags she'd brought on the trip with her and pulled out a small device.

She checked the room for any bugs or cameras that may have been left.

But there were none.

Once she put the device away, she turned to him. "Someone's been in here."

Carter felt certain of that also, but he couldn't put his finger on why. Nothing looked as if it had been touched. "How do you know?"

Ainsley glanced around again. "It's just a feeling, really. I'm still trying to pinpoint why exactly."

He shifted as he surveyed the room. "Ainsley . . . I don't like this. This whole thing is beginning to feel like a bad idea."

"We can't give up now. We're too close to finding answers."

"But . . ."

"We just need to be vigilant," Ainsley said. "Everything will be okay."

Everything will be okay . . .

Her words echoed in his mind as he set up his laptop.

She'd said those very words to him sixteen years ago. He'd been struggling with his future. Whether he should stay in college or drop out. If he should follow in his father's footsteps or go in his own direction. If he should please his family or possibly lose them.

He'd wrestled with the thoughts for so long.

He hadn't told many people about his personal crisis. But he'd told Ainsley.

She'd listened and offered no judgment.

When he'd finished talking, Ainsley had squeezed his arm and told him that, one way or another, it would all work out. She'd insisted he was smart, that he'd make the right choice. She'd said even if everything else fell through, he'd have her.

She'd grinned, almost as if joking.

She'd had no idea the immense comfort her words had offered.

How much that one conversation meant to him.

Carter blinked and tried to clear his thoughts as he turned back to the laptop.

Ainsley let out a long breath. "Now I say we try to figure out exactly what is on this hard drive."

"I can help with that." The two of them sat side by side on the couch as he began to decrypt the information on the hard drive.

CHAPTER
FORTY

AINSLEY LEANED OVER THE COMPUTER, anxious to see what may have been on Jack's hard drive.

Whatever it was, he thought it worth killing for.

Her arm brushed Carter's as she sat there, and she ignored the burst of warmth that spread through her. But her mind couldn't help but wander back to that kiss. She wasn't supposed to feel anything. Yet she did.

She was pretty sure that Carter felt something too based on the way he responded. It was almost as if they'd picked up where they'd left off sixteen years ago.

That could be a problem.

"Look at this," Carter muttered, tapping a few more keys on his laptop.

Pictures filled the screen.

Pictures of a man lip-locked with another woman.

There were several different shots of him.

Ainsley stared at him a moment before she realized who the man was.

Then she let out a breath. "That's the head of the FBI."

"And that's not his wife," Carter finished.

"Are you sure?"

He nodded. "I've met them before at a dinner. I'm sure."

Ainsley blinked several times as she processed that. "These are blackmail photos."

Carter looked at her and nodded. "That's at least partially what this is about. Someone is collecting trash on powerful people and using that to get what they want. Most likely, Jack and his crew are leveraging government grants. Maybe they're twisting the law so certain crimes they're associated with will be overlooked. They could even be manipulating votes in Congress."

"Having things like this would certainly give people a lot of leverage. It would probably even be something somebody would kill for. Someone like Jack Earl. Except he would probably have his guys do it for him."

"Maybe he even had something on Maureen. My dad. Everett. This is all tied in together, isn't it?"

"That's my best guess." She pulled out her phone. "I need to let Charlie know what's going on. Is there more or is this it?"

He looked at the screen. "There's more but it's behind the encryption. This looks like maybe it's the most recent addition so it's not behind all the firewalls like the other stuff."

"How long will it take to break through that encryption?"

Carter twisted his head. "That's a good question. I'll do what I can. But I've been working on picking up where my father left off."

She dialed Charlie's number and told her what they had discovered.

"This is big," Charlie said.

"Big enough that someone would stage a fake terrorist attack?" Ainsley asked.

"That's what we need to figure out. For now, I need you to stand down. We need to figure out more information on whatever is going on. It's bigger than the crew I have at the lodge. Understand?"

Ainsley had to fight the urge to do more. But she knew Charlie's words were true. They couldn't risk blowing this. Not when they had come so far.

"You just let me know what you need me to do," Ainsley said. "I'll be here in the meantime."

———

For now, it was a waiting game, Carter realized.

He had to figure out the rest of that encryption. But he didn't have to do it right here. They had the information they needed, and he just needed to figure out how to access it.

And he would.

But tension rippled through each of his muscles.

He and Ainsley had both changed out of their formal wear into more comfortable clothing, grabbed some waters, and returned to the couch. She needed to keep drinking water in order to flush any additional toxins out of her system. Both of their nerves appeared to be shot.

As Carter stared at her a moment, he remembered that kiss again.

Remembered the feel of her lips against his. Her sweet, flowery scent.

But mostly he remembered the passion that sparked between them.

It was something he would love to re-create again and again.

"Ainsley, about that kiss—"

"It was just a part of the cover," she quickly said.

Was she brushing it off as a protective measure? Carter had a feeling that was the case.

But . . .

"I'm not actually talking about the kiss from tonight. I'm talking about sixteen years ago. Could you at least try to listen to me? Please?"

She stared at him a moment before she finally nodded. "Okay."

He released a long breath. He had almost expected her to say no. But she hadn't. Now he needed to figure out where to start.

"As you probably know, Lillian and I dated for two years."

Her gaze narrowed. "I did hear something about that at some point."

"But right before I came to the ranch that summer, we broke up."

"You didn't really mention that in all of our talks."

"I'm not the type to kiss and tell. I don't like to talk about my relationships. I like to keep them between me and whoever I'm dating."

"Go on."

"I knew my relationship with Lillian wasn't going anywhere. She was more the type that my parents wanted me to date. She came from an affluent family.

She had good connections. But I didn't feel what I should for her."

Ainsley tucked her legs under her as she listened. She didn't say anything. She only waited.

"I didn't know she was coming to the rodeo that night. In fact, I was walking to get you some cotton candy. The blue stuff that you liked the most."

A small smile tugged at the edge of her lips.

"Before I even got there, Lillian showed up. And as I was asking her what she was doing there, she threw her arms around me and kissed me. I didn't know she'd be there. And I definitely didn't know she would kiss me."

"You could've pushed her away."

"If you had stuck around a moment longer, you would have seen that I did."

Ainsley crossed her arms. "Maybe that's true. I actually thought about that. Jason mentioned that maybe that could be the case. So I went to surprise you at college one weekend, and I saw the two of you holding hands. I figured maybe I wasn't reading too much into things after all."

Carter's eyes widened. "You came to see me?"

"I decided I was being petty and should listen to your explanation. Then I realized I was wrong." A frown tugged at her lips as if bad memories were pummeling her.

He started to reach for her, but he stopped himself. "I had no idea . . ."

She raised her chin stiffly. "Once I saw you together, I didn't want you to know I was there. It would've been even more humiliating."

"You wouldn't talk to me. I felt like I had blown it with you. And Lillian claimed that she had changed over the summer. She reminded me that we had two years together and shouldn't throw it all away. So I decided to give it another chance. Not right away. It took me some time."

"What happened?"

"We lasted about four months, and then I called things off. I knew that what happened between you and me was something much different than what I had with Lillian. I wanted what we had."

Ainsley rubbed her throat as she stared up at him. "Is that right?"

"I wanted to come see you again. Then Jason said that you had gone off to the academy to become a Ranger. He told me that you started dating someone else even."

"Ryan? It didn't last long."

"Is he the guy you brought to Jason's funeral?"

Her throat tightened even more. "Yes."

Carter shrugged. "I saw you there, and it just seemed like maybe I missed my opportunity."

The two of them stared at each other another moment, and Carter waited for Ainsley to call the next shot. He wasn't the one who needed to forgive her. He'd welcome Ainsley back into his life at the drop of a hat.

Right now, this decision rested solely on Ainsley.

AINSLEY STARED at Carter a moment as she considered his words.

He was telling the truth. She could hear it in his voice.

Had she been a fool for all these years?

Maybe.

But she'd seen what she'd seen. Maybe the timing just hadn't been right for them. If she'd been with Carter, would she have gone to the academy to become a Ranger?

She wasn't sure how life would have played out.

But she did know that the two of them were here now. Face-to-face.

Had they been given a second chance?

Perhaps.

"Carter . . ." She lifted her hand toward him.

And that was all it took.

The next instant, they were in each other's arms. Their lips met. Suddenly, all those years of repressed emotions exploded between them.

Ainsley knew they should take things slow.

But not yet.

Finally, she forced herself away from him and touched her swollen lips.

This was a horrible time to think about romance . . . but she'd be a fool to deny that something was growing between them.

Carter reached for her again, pushing a hair behind her ear as he stared at her with warmth in his gaze. "I've missed you so much, Ainsley. There's never really been anyone else like you."

"I feel the same way." She gently rubbed her thumb against his cheek.

She could sit here all day and stare at him.

As he leaned toward her and his lips brushed hers one more time, a knock sounded at the door.

The two of them jumped apart as if they had been caught doing something they shouldn't.

Ainsley stood and wiped her lips before straightening her outfit.

"Who could be here?" Carter asked.

"I have no idea." Ainsley grabbed her spare gun

and slipped it into her pocket. "Why don't you answer? I'll be right behind you."

———

Carter didn't want anything to interrupt the moment he and Ainsley had just shared. He wanted to relish it longer. Dwell on it. Relive it.

Besides, who could be here? Was it the person who'd been sending the roses?

He peered out the peephole and felt his shoulders tense. "It's Jack."

A knot formed between Ainsley's eyes. "Go ahead and answer."

As soon as he opened the door, Jack barged inside, acting as if he owned the place—maybe because he did.

"Sorry to stop by so late," he started.

Carter closed the door and exchanged a look with Ainsley. "It's okay. Is everything okay? I figured you'd be in bed by now."

"I was worried about you, Ainsley. Especially after everything that happened. I wanted to come check on you personally."

Was that really why he was here? Or did he know something? Did he suspect Ainsley had gotten her hands on that hard drive?

"I'm doing fine." Ainsley's voice sounded light and easygoing. "I appreciate your concern."

"You've got to know that what happened to you isn't normal here at my resort. I feel terribly about it." Jack's gaze lingered on her a moment longer than necessary.

What exactly was going through his mind?

"I don't blame you." Ainsley kept her hand in the front pocket of her hoodie where Carter knew the gun was.

She was cautious about all this, too, wasn't she?

He glanced around before his gaze stopped at the bed pillow on the couch.

If Jack saw it, it could make him wonder if the two of them weren't sleeping in the same bed.

Because they weren't.

But that didn't fit their cover story . . .

"I may or may not have gotten myself in the doghouse already," Carter explained.

Jack's eyebrows shot up. "Is that right?"

"We had a little tiff earlier, and I insisted I sleep on the couch. Don't worry. We've made up since then."

"I see." Jack's gaze continued to wander the room stopping at the desk.

Thankfully, Carter had put the computer and everything he'd brought with it away.

Otherwise, Jack could have been suspicious.

Finally, Jack turned his gaze back to them. "I thought I'd let you know we have what we believe is an additional visual on the man who abducted you— this one clearer than the one from the spa."

"What?" Ainsley clasped her hands together in front of her. "That's great news."

Jack pulled up something on his phone and showed it to them. "Does this man look familiar?"

Carter and Ainsley squeezed together to see.

He felt his eyes widen at the image there.

Hayes.

"I ran into that man in the lobby last night," Ainsley said. "He asked me for directions."

"And I ran into him when I was searching for Ainsley," Carter added. "He offered to help."

Jack frowned and nodded. "We checked security footage from around the lodge, and it looks like he's been following you."

Ainsley crossed her arms. "Did you catch this guy yet?"

"He was staying in the hall across from you under an assumed identity. I sent my guys there to question him, but he's gone."

Carter tried not to show his relief. Thankfully, Hayes hadn't been there. But they needed to warn him.

"I just wanted to let you know," Jack said. "We're going to keep searching for him. But in the meantime, you need to be on the lookout."

"We will be." Carter wrapped his arms around Ainsley like any concerned husband might. "I'm sorry this trip has turned into this."

Jack locked his gaze with Carter's. "Believe me, you're not nearly as sorry as I am."

His words hung in the air.

FORTY-TWO

AINSLEY COULD HARDLY WAIT until Jack left the room.

She locked the door behind him before letting out a long breath.

The good news was she hadn't had to use her gun.

But right now, she needed to warn Hayes.

There was no time to waste.

She paced from the door and grabbed her phone. Quickly, she dialed Hayes's number.

He didn't answer.

Carter stepped closer. "What's going on?"

"I don't know where Hayes could be. I don't know why he wouldn't be in his room, for that matter."

"Maybe he caught wind of this and fled."

"Maybe." Ainsley frowned as she nibbled on her bottom lip. "But I have a bad feeling in the pit of my stomach. I want to make sure he knows what's going on."

"Do you think Jack knows what we're doing?"

Ainsley's shoulders tensed even more. "I'm not sure. It was suspicious that he came here. I saw him looking around, almost like he knew something. But we've covered our tracks. He shouldn't know any of this."

Carter's hand came down on her shoulder, and he squeezed it. "Just take a deep breath. We've got this."

His calm reassurance did make her feel better. It had always had that effect on her. Both exciting her and making her feel grounded at the same time.

It was quite the combination.

She glanced at her phone again. "I'm going to try to call Hayes one more time. But if he doesn't answer, I'm going to have to go look for him."

"Jack will probably see you."

"Then I'll come up with some type of excuse. But I can't let one of my colleagues be hurt. Not if I'm capable of stopping it."

She dialed his number again.

This time, Hayes answered.

"Ainsley . . ." Hayes nearly sounded breathless. "This isn't good."

"I know," she whispered. "They're looking for you."

"I know. I'm—"

But before he could finish the sentence, shouts sounded on the other end of the line.

"Hayes?" Ainsley gripped the phone harder.

But there was no response.

The line went dead.

Something terrible had just happened.

Ainsley was certain of it.

———

Carter didn't like the way any of this was going.

He had a feeling it would get worse before it got better.

"I've got to go out there and find him." Ainsley still gripped her phone so hard that Carter feared it might break.

As she stepped toward the door, he grabbed her arm. "That's a bad idea."

"I can't leave him out there hanging out to dry."

"What are you going to tell people when they ask why you're wandering around at this time of night?"

"I can just say I'm stretching my legs. I can go for a jog to burn some energy off. I don't know. But I can't wait in here any longer."

"Let's go for a jog together. I think they might buy that as an excuse. But I'm going with you, okay?"

"Carter, you're not trained to—"

"No, I'm not trained to be a bodyguard like you are. But I have good instincts. I'm not going to get myself killed."

Ainsley only stared at him a moment before nodding. "Okay. Let's go."

Five minutes later, they'd changed into jogging clothes and were heading toward the lodge lobby.

He glanced around as they walked.

He halfway expected to see Jack's guys scurrying around.

He expected police or ambulances.

After all, something had happened with Hayes.

"Let's head toward the parking lot," Ainsley said.

Carter sensed her nerves. She didn't like this. Even though she'd tucked a gun underneath her shirt, they still didn't really know what they were up against here.

But when they reached the parking lot, there was no sign of unusual activity.

"Where could Hayes be?"

"I think I can find his car," Ainsley whispered. "I'm going to jog through the lot. But you stay here. It won't look right if we're both wandering the parking lot right now."

Carter didn't like the sound of that, but he nodded.

A moment later, Ainsley jogged away.

Almost no sooner had she left did he feel someone beside him.

Prancer.

"I'm surprised that I'm running into you again," Prancer said.

"Same here. I figured you'd all be turning in for the night."

"I just needed some fresh air."

"I understand that."

Prancer turned to him and lowered his voice. "While we're here, just you and I, I wanted to know if you've considered the offer?"

In the middle of all this, Prancer was going to talk about a job offer?

Carter shouldn't be surprised.

"I'm still thinking it over," Carter said. "I'll have an answer for you tomorrow."

Prancer grinned and clamped Carter's arm with his hand. "Very well. That's exactly what we want to hear."

CHAPTER
FORTY-THREE

HAYES'S CAR was still here.

But there was no one inside.

Quietly, Ainsley called Charlie and gave her an update.

She put her phone away and turned to find Carter again when Jack appeared.

Her nerves quaked at the sight of him, but she quickly pulled herself together and smiled.

"Jack . . . I wasn't expecting to see you out here."

"The local police are on their way. I wanted to wait out here for them."

"I see." She glanced in the distance, wishing she could get back to Carter.

Jack stepped closer and lowered his voice. "I'm quite concerned about you."

"About me?" She pointed to herself. "You don't need to be. I'm fine."

He touched her arm, and she wanted to withdraw. But she didn't. She kept her gaze steady.

However, unease jostled inside her.

"You have a potential stalker here. A new marriage with a highly successful man who's a certified bachelor."

Her eyebrows shot up. "A certified bachelor?"

"Everyone knows Carter is quite the womanizer."

"I don't know about that . . ." She couldn't believe she was defending Carter. But she was.

"You're a lovely, lovely woman, Ainsley." His voice came out soft, almost sultry.

Before she realized what was happening, Jack leaned toward her and pressed his lips into hers.

She startled before pushing him away. "What are you doing?"

He didn't look the slightest bit embarrassed as he stared at her. "Did I misread you?"

"Yes. I'm married." She wiped her lips, trying to erase the feel of Jack's mouth against hers. "You know that."

He shrugged. "I've seen the way you look at me."

She was looking at him like that because she wondered if he was guilty. But she couldn't tell him that.

"Why don't we pretend that didn't happen," Jack said. "It won't happen again."

If Carter knew about this . . . he might break cover in order to give Jack a piece of his mind. She didn't want that.

"Okay—let's pretend this didn't happen." Ainsley took a step back. "I need to find Carter now."

Before he could say anything else, she hurried away.

———

Ainsley joined Carter a moment later, trying not to give away the fact that anything was wrong.

But what had just happened?

Did Jack really think she'd wanted him to kiss her?

She found that hard to believe.

Then again, Jack was the type of man who got anything and everything he wanted.

The whole encounter left her feeling shaken.

Carter studied her face as she got closer. "Everything okay?"

Instinctively, she gravitated toward his arms. But this time it wasn't because of their charade.

It was because it felt natural.

"Yes, of course."

He squinted and studied her face. "You're trembling some."

Before he could respond, she heard a footstep behind them.

She turned and saw Jack had followed her.

She felt herself tense at the sight of him.

"I'm glad I ran into you both," Jack started. "I wanted to mention our plans for tomorrow. I would love for you to come visit Heaven."

Her eyebrows shoved up higher. "What was that?"

Had he just threatened them?

His grin widened. "It's the name of a personal lodge I have at the top of the mountain. It's only for me and my VIP guests. I would love for us to spend our last full day here in Heaven."

All kinds of grisly thoughts crept through her mind. She hoped her face did not show any of them. She nodded.

"That sounds amazing," she said.

"Great."

As she and Carter walked back into the resort, she leaned closer and whispered, "I can't find Hayes anywhere."

She froze as gunfire cut through the air in the distance.

CHAPTER
FORTY-FOUR

CARTER STIFFENED AT THE SOUND.

He slipped his arm around Ainsley and pulled her toward him.

Even though the gunfire sounded like it was far away, he couldn't take any chances.

They paused and turned around.

Jack put his phone to his ear as he walked briskly inside.

Carter waited, hoping the man would share an update.

He paused, said more things into his phone, and then turned to them.

"I suppose you both just heard that sound," he said.

"Is everything okay?" Carter pulled Ainsley closer.

"I'd say yes. It's actually very good for you. My guys have just shot the man who abducted you from the spa."

Carter sucked in a tight breath as he turned to Ainsley. She looked equally as shocked.

"The man from the photos? The one who was helping Carter look for me?"

"No, we haven't been able to locate him. But we believe he was working with somebody."

"And they shot him?" Ainsley's voice crept with tension.

"At first, they were just going to talk to him. But then he pulled out a weapon and—"

"Is he still . . . alive?" Ainsley asked.

"Unfortunately, it doesn't appear so. But an ambulance is on the way now. So I will know more soon."

"Will the police come?" Carter asked. "Will they need to question Ainsley?"

"The police are already on their way. I'm sure they will need to investigate. But I'm hoping that you will be able to sleep a little better tonight knowing that this guy won't be roaming the lodge."

"And the other man?" Carter asked. "Do you still believe that he's guilty?"

"We're still considering him a person of interest. My guys will keep looking for him."

"Good to know," Ainsley murmured. "I appreciate the fact that you jumped on this."

"Of course. No one messes with the people in my circle. I need to make sure everybody knows that."

His words had an ominous ring to them.

Ainsley didn't say anything until they were back in their suite. But as soon as the door was locked and they had moved away from it, she turned to Carter.

"I don't like this," she announced.

"Do you think they have Hayes?"

"I have no idea. It doesn't make sense that he's not answering his phone. What if they didn't really shoot the guy who abducted me, but they shot Hayes?"

"What do you want to do?" Carter asked.

"I talked to Charlie. She said we shouldn't blow our cover yet. That she is going to handle this. But they are a long way away. And I'm not."

"If you go out there and search for Hayes, then people are going to get suspicious. From what I know about Hayes, he's a professional. He knows what he's doing."

"He is . . . but even the most professional operative can still run into danger."

"I will support you whatever you want to do."

His words brought her a strange comfort.

Most guys wanted to call the shots themselves. She'd been around that all too often. Even among her colleagues.

She thought about it a moment and tried to keep her thoughts and rationale under control.

Finally, she nodded and let out a long breath. "You need to work on seeing if you can break that encryption. I'm going to call Charlie one more time. But for now, I need to trust her. And trust that she is on this and that there's nothing I should do. I'll let her make that call . . . but I don't like any of this."

Carter pulled her into a lingering hug. "Me neither. Me neither."

AINSLEY AND CARTER stayed up most of the night.

Carter continued to work on figuring out the encryption that his father had created.

Meanwhile, Ainsley was on the phone with Charlie, trying to figure out what happened to Hayes.

There had been no updates.

It seemed as if Hayes had disappeared off the face of the earth.

Her soul felt unsettled at the thought of it.

She wanted more than anything to be out there helping her colleague.

But Charlie had two more operatives checking into the resort this morning who were going to help out. The roads had been closed, but somehow, they managed to get through.

Ainsley prayed Hayes had simply run and hidden until backup arrived. That nothing had happened to him.

Still, she could feel the danger closing in.

She wasn't looking forward to going to Heaven today.

She thought she was isolated here at this resort. But taking a private ski lift up to a lodge at the top of a mountain would be even more secluded.

If Jack became suspicious, there would be no one to rely on except herself.

She glanced at Carter as he leaned back on the couch, appearing exhausted as his eyes closed and he rubbed his neck.

Maybe they shouldn't go. Or maybe only she should go, and she should tell them that Carter wasn't feeling well. Maybe they should just get out of here and figure out another plan.

They had the hard drive now. So what were they trying to prove? Carter just needed to figure out the encryption key.

"Why are you looking at me like that?" Carter raised his head slightly.

Ainsley walked across the room and sat beside him. "I don't want you to go up there today."

He sat up straighter, and his gaze locked with hers. "I'll be okay."

"There are no guarantees in this, Carter."

"I know. I feel the same way about you. I'm also worried that something could happen to you."

"So what are we going to do?"

"We have to do what we came here to do," Carter said. "Someone has to stop these guys. We've been placed here at the right time and place. For everything, there is a season. This is ours."

Ainsley's gaze caught with his. "Are you sure you're up for this?"

"Not really. But I'm going to do it. That's what you do when the right opportunity arises."

She leaned forward and pressed her lips to his. "I've always known there was a reason I liked you."

He raked his hands through her hair. "And I've always known there's a reason I loved you."

Ainsley's breath caught. "What?"

He rested his hand on the side of her face. "It's true. There's never been anyone like you."

Ainsley opened her mouth, feeling as if she should return the sentiment. But did she love Carter? Or was she just setting herself up for more heartache right now?

Instead of answering, she pressed another kiss on his lips.

When she pulled back, she said, "We need to get a

little sleep, then we've got to get ready. We've got a big day ahead of us."

Carter's gaze lingered on her another moment before he finally nodded. "Yes, we do."

———

Carter felt the apprehension thrumming through him when they awoke.

He and Ainsley met Eric outside, and he escorted them to the private ski lift.

"This will take you to the top, and there will be someone up there to help you get off," Eric explained. "I'm sure you both know the drill."

Carter stared up at the ski lift. There were probably only six double-bench seats on the whole thing, and it led up a steep incline. No one else was on it right now.

This had bad idea written all over it.

Ainsley turned to Eric as they waited for their bench. "By the way, any updates on last night?"

Eric shook his head. "Not that I've heard. I know the one guy was pronounced dead. But as far as the other guy—the one from the photos? No one has been able to find him."

Before they got on the ski lift, Eric turned toward

them. The way he fidgeted made him seem nervous —and like he had something on his mind.

"Everything okay?" Ainsley asked.

"I may be looking for another job when this is all done," he started. "If you need an assistant, let me know."

"Why would you look for another job?" Carter asked, curiosity pulsing through him.

He stepped closer. "I think Haley set you up at the spa."

Ainsley's eyebrows shot up. "Why would you say that?"

"I saw her talking to Katie, the lady who did your wrap. I know she had her sights set on Carter. I overheard her talking to Brooke and Joy about him. I think she wanted to send Ainsley home so she could move in."

Carter processed that a moment. "Thank you for sharing that. I had no idea."

"It seems only fair to let you know."

Carter stepped closer. "How long have you worked for Jack?"

"A long time. But I'm not sure how much longer. People around him keep turning up dead. I don't want to be next." He clamped his mouth shut. "I shouldn't have said that. But most of the people he surrounds himself with are so spineless. You two seem different. Please don't tell him I said this."

"We won't." Carter locked his gaze with Eric's. "But maybe you should look for another job before it's too late."

"I'm not sure I'll ever be able to walk away . . ."

Carter would have to think more about that later.

Right now, he hoped this meeting would provide some answers.

But they were going to need to proceed very carefully.

A moment later, Carter and Ainsley were sitting on the lift, a thin bar in front of them as they headed toward the lodge at the top.

Carter sucked in a cool breath, grateful for his warm coat.

"What do you think of that?" Ainsley asked.

"He seemed sincere."

"I agree. He looked scared too, didn't he?"

"I would be. If Jack knows Eric is doubting him, he'll be the next one to have a tragic accident."

Silence fell for a minute.

Carter glanced around, trying to clear his head. "It really is beautiful up here. The irony, right? We're in one of the most beautiful places on earth, in my opinion, and yet there's so much ugliness around us."

"Sounds like a good analogy about life. Beautiful yet ugly. Very rarely is something all one or the other."

"Except you." Carter leaned toward Ainsley until their foreheads met. "You're all beautiful."

Ainsley let out a soft laugh. "Aren't you charming?"

"Isn't it only charm if it's not true?"

She looked up at him with a look in her eyes that took his breath away.

He planted a quick kiss on her lips before pulling away. Even though she hadn't told him she loved him, he was patient. He could wait.

For now, he slipped his arm around her as they rode up the mountain.

Just then, his phone buzzed.

He almost ignored it, but something made him glance at his screen.

He'd gotten a picture.

From the same number as earlier.

He squinted as he glanced at it.

When it opened, he saw the photo of Ainsley and . . . Jack.

And they were kissing.

FORTY-SIX

"WHAT'S WRONG?" Ainsley sensed that whatever message Carter had just gotten wasn't good.

He glanced at her, an unreadable look in his eyes. "How could you?"

She twisted her head. "How could I what?"

He showed her his phone screen. "You and Jack?"

Ainsley's eyes widened as her breath left her lungs. "It's not what you think."

"This was last night. Did you secretly go out and meet with him? Is this some kind of revenge?"

"Carter . . ." She licked her lips. "I can explain . . ."

"I had a feeling I couldn't trust you. That you were hiding something." He shook his head, a dumbfounded look on his face. "I should have listened to my instincts."

"Jack kissed me!" Ainsley blurted. "I pushed him away and asked him what he was doing. He must have cornered me just to get this picture. He wants to hold it over me."

"What? Why would he do that?" Carter stared at her with doubt.

"You know his game," Ainsley said. "He probably had it all planned."

"Even if that's true . . . why didn't you tell me?"

"I feared if you knew he'd kissed me that you might blow our cover. I couldn't risk that."

As Carter stared at her, Ainsley wondered what he was thinking.

Did he believe her?

Or did he think she was in on all this also?

———

Carter stared at Ainsley, trying to sort out his feelings.

Could he trust her?

He wanted to.

He really did.

But he'd gotten burned before.

So had she.

And Jack Earl was manipulative. Carter wouldn't put it past him to plan something like this.

Still . . . why hadn't she told him?

And there was something else that was bothering him . . .

"So, this is all about our cover?" He stared at her as cold air nipped at his nose. "This is about you and us maintaining our fake relationship and getting answers? Is that still all this is to you?"

"Carter . . . no." Ainsley frowned. "You've got to know this assignment has become so much more to me."

"I'm not sure about anything anymore. I know you're determined. That you don't let anything slow you down. Maybe I'm the one who's been a fool here. This was just part of the job, wasn't it?"

"Carter . . ."

Before she could finish her statement, the ski lift lurched.

Everything happened so fast that Carter didn't have time to react.

Instead, he watched helplessly as Ainsley jerked forward and slipped under the safety bar.

Then she toppled toward the ground.

EVERYTHING HAD HAPPENED in a split second.

The ski lift stopped suddenly.

Ainsley slid.

Felt herself falling.

The air left her lungs.

Her arms flailed.

She'd looked up and saw Carter staring at her with alarm.

Her hand caught onto the edge of the bench.

The downward momentum stopped as she jerked to a halt.

Instead of plummeting to the rugged ground below, she dangled, her hand barely gripping the cold metal.

She grasped the seat with her other hand.

"Hold on!" Carter shouted.

He lifted the safety bar and shifted his weight as he leaned toward her, clearly trying to keep his balance and not shift the bench too much.

Ainsley glanced down and saw the snow beneath her—far beneath her.

She'd probably survive this fall.

But when her body collided with the snow, it wouldn't feel good.

It wouldn't be pretty.

Her hands began slipping, and she cried out.

"Don't let go!" Carter grabbed her wrists.

Just as Carter began to lift her, the ski lift sprang to life again.

They both jolted.

Carter nearly toppled over the edge, almost losing his hold on her wrists.

He righted himself and scooted back before muttering beneath his breath. Then his grasp on her wrists tightened.

"It's going to be okay," he murmured.

Somehow, he sounded so convincing as he said the words.

He angled his body and wrapped his legs around Ainsley. Then he leaned back and lifted her toward him.

The extra momentum gave her enough leverage

to grasp onto the back of the ski lift, and she pulled herself up onto the seat.

But the actions made Carter start to slip forward.

Ainsley quickly lowered the safety bar, keeping him from sliding out also.

She was a trembling mess by the time they were both safe again.

Lifts had never been her favorite thing.

Now she knew why.

Despite their earlier fight, Carter pulled her into his arms. "Are you okay?"

"I am now . . . I just hope that that wasn't a sign of things to come."

The ski lift stopping . . . it hadn't been on accident, had it?

———

If Carter had his way, he would continue taking the ski lift back down to the resort. Then, when they got there, he and Ainsley could leave.

But he remembered their talk last night.

Remembered that they were the ones who'd been put in this position and equipped to find out some answers.

These guys had gotten away with things for entirely too long.

They needed to be stopped before more damage could be done.

That image of the head of the FBI was just the start of this. If Jack and his gang could manipulate the head of the FBI, that gave them a lot of power.

Too much power.

Corrupt men could not get away with doing corrupt things. It had happened nearly since the beginning of time.

Until heroes had risen up to put an end to it.

Carter didn't consider himself a hero. But he would do everything within his power to stop this.

Especially since he had the means of figuring this out.

He just had to decipher his father's encryption code.

If only there was a way that Ainsley wouldn't get caught in the middle of the crossfire right now.

He knew how much he cared about her—despite everything that had happened.

But he still wasn't sure about her feelings for him.

Finally, they reached the top of the lift. A worker waited there and helped them off.

"I don't know what happened back there," the man said. "Glad you're okay. There must have been some kind of glitch. That usually doesn't happen."

"Thankfully, it turned out okay," Carter muttered.

But he wasn't so sure that was a glitch.

They found their balance a moment before staring at the lodge in the distance.

The place was everything that Carter had expected it to be. Beautiful with lots of tall windows and hefty wood beams. No expense had been spared.

He took Ainsley's hand as they started toward the door.

"Are you ready for this?" he asked.

She stared at it another moment before nodding, a new determination in her gaze. "Let's do this."

AINSLEY KNEW THE STAKES.

But they weren't going to be able to turn back now.

She wouldn't even if she could.

These people had to be stopped before anyone else got hurt.

Instead, she gripped Carter's hand harder as they stepped into the lodge.

When they got inside, she was surprised she didn't see anyone else here.

She assumed the rest of the board members would be here.

Besides, it wasn't as if Ainsley and Carter were early.

They were right on time.

Maybe everyone else was in another room.

In the meantime, some coffee and pastries had been left out.

She glanced around, soaking in the cozy space.

This place wasn't your typical ski lodge. Yes, it was built from milled logs. A huge stone fireplace stretched up one wall, and leather couches were artfully arranged.

But directly overhead, there was a large—a gigantic—aquarium suspended from the ceiling. Four other aquariums also graced the room, an interesting mix of beach life versus mountain chalet.

She and Carter wandered toward the pastry table.

Were the other operatives from Vanishing Ranch at the lodge yet?

If so, how would they get up here to help if needed? All the questions flooded her mind.

The ski lift was really the only viable way to get up here. Unless maybe there was a back road leading to this chalet.

That had to be it. They hadn't been able to build this chalet by carrying equipment up on a ski lift.

Still, the whole situation left Ainsley feeling unnerved.

She glanced around again.

Where were Jack and the rest of the gang?

"Something feel funny right now to you?" Carter asked.

"Very." If she didn't see someone soon, they'd get back on that ski lift, go back down, and assume a miscommunication had happened.

They would run into Jack later and explain the situation. She'd feel much better fighting this battle at the lodge than up here anyway.

She poured a cup of coffee that she didn't intend to drink. As she turned, she heard a footstep behind her.

She fully expected to see Jack.

Instead, she nearly dropped her coffee when she saw the familiar figure standing there.

Was that . . . Lillian?

———

Carter stared at the woman in front of them.

"Lillian?" Surprise stretched through his voice. "What are you doing here?"

She grinned and stepped closer. She wore black ski bibs with a long-sleeved white top beneath it. Her silky dark hair was swept back in a twist, and her eyes glimmered with pleasure.

"It's good to see you again too, Carter." She

glanced at Ainsley and nodded. "It's like a big reunion right now, isn't it?"

Carter twisted his head, not liking this.

Not liking how Ainsley released his hand and seemed to withdraw more with every second that passed.

"What are you doing here?" he repeated.

"You didn't know?" Her eyes sparkled with smugness. "I work for Jack."

"Since when?"

"I have for the past couple of years. I thought you knew."

"The two of us don't really keep up."

Her eyebrows flickered up as she grinned. "No, we don't, do we? But I love the way things come full circle."

"Speaking of Jack . . . where is he?" A new hardness entered Ainsley's voice.

"He'll be with you in a second. He asked me to come out and make sure that everything was okay first."

"Have you been here at the chalet this whole time?" Carter asked.

"I just arrived last night. I was on an overseas business trip, but I got here as soon as I could. Jack thought that maybe it would be better if I wasn't here right away anyway." She leaned closer. "You know. Considering our history and everything."

Carter rolled his shoulders back. "I don't like this game that you seem to be playing right now, Lillian."

Some of the smugness left her gaze. "Game? Don't flatter yourself."

Carter didn't know what was going on here.

But whatever it was, he didn't like it.

AINSLEY TRIED NOT to burn a hole in Lillian with her gaze.

But she didn't believe in coincidences.

The fact that Lillian worked for Jack set off major alarms in her head.

Had Jack known about the history between Lillian and Carter and hired her because of that?

Or did this whole scheme go that far back? Had Lillian been planted in Carter's life all those years ago to fulfill some type of purpose?

That would have been fifteen years ago. Around the time of the terrorist bombing. Back then, Doyle had known Jack. Was there some type of connection they were missing?

It was a possibility. One Ainsley hadn't considered before.

There was clearly more to the story.

Lillian's phone buzzed, and she glanced at it before smiling again. "Jack will see you now."

Carter and Ainsley took a step toward the hallway Lillian had emerged from.

Lillian raised a finger to stop them. "Just Carter."

"What do you mean?" Carter narrowed his gaze.

"Jack only wants to see you."

Carter shook his head. "We're a package deal. If I go, she goes. And where is everyone else?"

"They're coming. Don't worry. Jack just wanted to talk to you for a moment first. That's just the way he does things sometimes."

"I'm not leaving Ainsley." He planted his feet where he stood.

"I'll be okay. I'll just wait here in the lobby, right?" Ainsley glanced at Lillian.

"That's right. She can wait here. I'll make sure she's taken care of."

Ainsley wasn't sure she liked the sound of that.

She *could* take care of herself.

It was Carter she worried about.

Especially when she looked at Lillian's eyes.

Jack knew who Ainsley really was, didn't he?

She glanced around and saw several security guards had appeared.

That's when she knew she and Carter didn't have much choice right now but to cooperate.

———

He and Ainsley should have left while they could.

That was all Carter could think about.

But now they were here.

Trapped.

There was no way to get past the security guards at the door. Even if they did, they couldn't exactly take the ski lift back down.

The situation was getting worse and worse by the moment.

Carter took one last lingering glance at Ainsley before following Lillian down the hallway to meet Jack.

"You and I both know it's not a coincidence that we're both here," Carter said.

Lillian looked at him, that smugness returning to her gaze. "I don't know what you're talking about. I'm the one who's worked for Jack for the past couple of years. You're the one who just showed up. So if anything, it appears you arranged this meeting."

"In your dreams," he muttered.

"Say what you want." She opened the door. "I hope y'all enjoy your meeting, though."

Carter glared at her another moment before stepping into the room.

Jack waited at the end of the conference table.

By himself.

A computer sat in front of him.

As the door closed, the security guard moved in front of it.

Carter shifted uncomfortably. "What's going on here?"

Jack's lips flickered as if he wanted to grin but didn't. "I need you to finish the encryption work that your father began."

"What makes you think I can do that?"

"Because I know you have the ability to do that. It's important to me."

"Why can't Ainsley be in here with me?"

"Because she can't." Jack reached into his pocket and placed something on the table.

Carter's breath caught.

It was Ainsley's gun.

"What's that?" Carter asked, playing dumb.

"It's the gun that was used to shoot that man last night. Turns out, he wasn't the one who abducted Ainsley. But one of my guys found this gun, and we're going to report it to the police. It just so happens that Ainsley was in the parking lot about the time that shot went off. The gun has her prints all over it, and she is the one with the motive to kill this guy. At the time, she thought he was the one terrorizing her."

"Jack . . ." Carter's voice held warning.

"No one messes with me." Jack's voice hardened. "Only if they want me to ruin them. Most people don't want that."

Carter's gaze locked on his. "You killed my father, didn't you?"

"All he had to do was finish this encryption work and give me the key. He told me he had when, in fact he'd locked down information I needed. I didn't realize that in time."

"You thought you had everything you needed from him, so you murdered him. Then you realized you should have kept him alive longer. You had important information that you could no longer retrieve."

Jack scowled. "That's right. And now I need you to finish the work that your father started."

AINSLEY AND LILLIAN stared at each other.

Ainsley was the first to speak. "What are you really doing here?"

Lillian flicked her gaze as if dismissing Ainsley. "My job."

Ainsley crossed her arms. "And what exactly is your job?"

"Whatever Jack tells me to do."

Ainsley wasn't buying any of this. There was clearly more to the story. "I thought you cared about Carter."

Her eyes narrowed with annoyance. "I did at one time. But I moved on. I could tell that he never got over you."

Ainsley glanced around the room, wondering

where Carter was and what Jack was talking to him about.

She had a feeling it wasn't anything good.

In fact, she could feel danger closing in.

"You should just leave them be," Lillian said, almost as if reading her thoughts.

Ainsley stared her dead in the eye. "That's exactly what you would like, isn't it? What are you planning to do in Dallas?"

Surprise flashed through her gaze. "I don't know what you're talking about."

"Don't play dumb. You guys are planning something else at the summit in Dallas. World leaders will be there. Are you going to plant another bomb?"

"Don't be stupid."

But Ainsley had seen the flash of fear in her gaze.

She was onto something.

She glanced around, trying to formulate a plan.

"If you're thinking about running, you'll never get out of here," Lillian said.

Ainsley couldn't argue that. She was stuck at the top of a mountain. Snow-filled slopes surrounded her.

If she tried to run, she'd probably just break her neck.

She glanced around the room one more time and counted three guards—including one who was the man she'd seen Jack whispering to the first night they'd arrived.

There was one guard at each door.

Ready to act.

With holstered guns at their waist.

Ainsley frowned.

The situation was going to be very tricky.

———

Carter sat at the computer, pretending to work on cracking the encryption key.

But he couldn't do this.

As soon as Jack had the information that he needed, people would be hurt.

There was no way that Jack had any intention of keeping him and Ainsley alive after this. They knew too much. They could ruin him.

No doubt there would be some type of tragic skiing accident that would make people easily believe that their deaths hadn't been homicides. When the ski lift had stopped earlier that had probably just been a warning. Jack had taken a chance, anticipating Carter and Ainsley wouldn't truly be harmed.

He'd almost been wrong.

Carter stared at the computer and frowned.

Maybe there was something Carter could do to send a message to somebody under the guise of working on this encryption.

"Don't try anything." Jack's voice cut through his thoughts. "I have it set up so that if you try any strange, tricky key strokes, we'll be alerted."

Carter narrowed his eyes. He should've figured Jack would realize that. But Carter had been hoping for the best.

He hit a few more keys before glancing at Jack. "When did you know?"

"Before you came. I put a bug on your phone."

"My phone is encrypted."

"My guys are good. Just not as good as your dad. Maybe not as good as you. But we do have a few tricks up our sleeves."

Carter stared at him another moment. "Did you have something to do with the bombings in Florida fifteen years ago?"

Something flashed in Jack's eyes, but he said nothing.

Carter could read into that. He knew that Jack was involved. This was all connected somehow.

Was the content of these files all the key?

"Why did you kill Maureen?" Carter continued, buying a little bit of time.

"To send a message to you, of course. I had to let

you know that you were in over your head. That I was in control."

"You were the one leaving those roses, weren't you?" He might as well find out some information.

"I've been keeping my eye on anyone who looked into the bombing in Florida," Jack said. "Including Ainsley. In fact, I was the one who told Dante that Ainsley liked him and that he should go after her."

"What?" Carter couldn't believe what he was hearing.

"I couldn't make him do anything, of course. But I monitored the situation. I thought he was going to kill her and get her out of my hair. But she was too smart and brave for that. However, it's not too late to correct my mistakes."

"So you knew Ainsley was coming with me?" Carter was trying to make the pieces fit.

"I knew someone was coming. I had one of my guys watching. When I saw it was Ainsley, I had him go buy the rose. It all worked out so beautifully really."

"And Everett? Was he your handiwork as well?"

Jack's eyes narrowed.

He hadn't expected Carter to make the connection, had he?

He didn't want people to know about his involvement with Everett's death.

The next instant, Jack reached into his pocket and pulled out a gun.

Before Carter could react, Jack smacked it across his face.

Pain raced down his jaw, and he let out a grunt.

"Enough talking!" Jack muttered. "Now work!"

AINSLEY STARED BACK AT LILLIAN, her thoughts still racing.

She could run and try to get to Carter.

But it would do no good.

She was outnumbered, and these people would catch her.

In the meantime, maybe she should simply try to find out more answers.

"You knew Carter kissed me at the rodeo, didn't you?" Ainsley started. "You sabotaged us."

Based on the smirk on Lillian's face, Ainsley had hit the nail on the head.

"Were you targeting Carter even back then?"

"Not really. But I know how to work things to my advantage."

Ainsley's gaze flickered around the room again.

She had a gun tucked into her jacket. Of course, she had brought more than one with her. The puffy jacket she wore seemed to conceal it perfectly. If only she could reach in there and get it without anyone noticing.

As she heard a yell from the other room, her breath caught.

What was going on?

She looked around one more time.

Then her gaze flickered outside where she saw movement.

Movement?

Her breath caught.

It was Hayes.

She was certain of it.

He was here. He was close. He'd be able to help.

But was anyone else from Vanishing Ranch here?

Ainsley wasn't sure.

She was still going to have to plan her next moves very carefully.

———

Carter's jaw throbbed, but he stared at the computer anyway.

Just what had his father done for this encryption?

Then a conversation flipped back in his mind. A conversation where his father had mentioned a cipher. He'd said he was going to use one for everyone to find their Christmas gifts that year. Then he'd handed them a family photo.

When Carter had accidentally broken the frame, he'd found a handwritten note on the back of it—a note that didn't exactly make sense.

It was because that was the cipher.

The information he needed in order to break through this encryption and find that information.

"You remembered something," Jack said. "I can see it on your face."

Carter swallowed hard, not wanting to admit that was the truth.

"Whatever you just remembered, I need you to use it. I need that information."

Carter had to make a quick decision. If he used the encryption key, then Jack would have what he wanted. No doubt he had a lot of plans for this information and what he wanted to do with it.

Would giving him the information now buy Carter time? Would he be able to stop whatever plan Jack put into place later?

Or would he just be setting himself up for an early death?

He wasn't sure.

He had to decide quickly.

But before he could, gunfire sounded in the other room.

His breath caught.

Ainsley . . . was she okay?

AINSLEY ONLY HAD a split second to act.

She hoped she didn't regret it.

But she remembered her advice from her bull-riding days. *Stay centered. Stay focused. Stay in sync with the bull.*

That had always been the key to succeeding when she wanted to ride for eight seconds and win.

She probably had approximately eight seconds to succeed right now also.

As Hayes threw a rock at the window and distracted the guards, Ainsley grabbed the gun from her jacket. She shot the shoulder of the man behind her.

Then the knee of the man on the other side of her.

Before she could shoot the third man, Lillian tackled her.

The two wrestled on the floor.

As they did, the third guard started to rush toward them.

Ainsley aimed her gun and shot again.

Her bullet hit his knee also.

Lillian grabbed her hand and slammed it into the floor.

The gun slid across the floor out of reach.

Ainsley pulled herself back and rose to her feet.

So did Lillian.

As the two women faced off, someone stepped from the hallway.

Two people.

Jack and Carter.

Ainsley glanced over.

Jack had a gun to Carter's head.

She instantly froze.

———

"Don't listen to anything he says." Carter felt the veins at his temples bulging as the gun pressed into his head.

Ainsley's gaze shot to him, alarm racing through her eyes.

"He needs to be taken down," Carter continued.

"Jack can*not* walk away from this scot-free. He can't continue doing what he's been doing."

"I'll shoot him," Jack muttered, his nostrils flaring. "Not enough to kill him. But to hurt him. To make him suffer. Don't test me."

Three guards were down. Each of them suffering from gunshot wounds. All disabled.

Two more guards ran into the chalet. Carter wasn't sure where they had come from.

But they were armed.

And Ainsley wasn't.

Carter's gaze flickered to the floor, and he saw her gun there.

He'd seen her and Lillian sparring in the center of the floor—a sight he never thought he would see.

"You've got to know you're out numbered," Jack continued. "I've already arranged a tragic ski accident that's going to happen. Or you can do what we say, and no one will be hurt."

"You were the one behind all of this, weren't you?" Ainsley asked. "You sent the flowers and texts. You killed Maureen and planted that detonator."

A satisfied grin twitched at Jack's lips. "I don't know what you're talking about."

But he did. Carter had no doubt about that.

He'd been pulling all the strings here. That was simply what Jack Earl did.

"Enough talking!" Jack growled. "We have business to take care of."

Carter tried to send mental communication to Ainsley that she shouldn't listen.

They couldn't let Jack and his guys win.

As Ainsley's gaze connected with his, he saw that determination in her . . . the same determination he'd seen right before she had gone on to win that bull-riding championship.

He didn't know what Ainsley was thinking, but she definitely had a plan.

CHAPTER
FIFTY-THREE

AINSLEY HAD TO MAKE A DECISION. She needed to do it now.

"You need to convince Carter to cooperate," Jack crooned. "For everyone's sake. You know this won't end well. You're outnumbered. Just be a good girl."

"You know what they say," Ainsley started.

When she didn't continue, Jack let out an irritated grunt and said, "What's that?"

"Well-behaved women rarely make history."

The next instant, Ainsley grabbed a gun from her ankle holster, pointed it at the ceiling, and pulled the trigger.

She barely had time to dive out of the way before glass and water—and fish—cascaded all over the place.

But she hoped that distraction bought them enough time to escape.

As cold water and glass shards covered her, she looked back.

Was Carter okay?

Ainsley sucked in a breath when she saw him elbow Jack in the face. Grab his gun.

The water had been just enough of a distraction that Carter was able to make a move.

Then Ainsley's gaze flipped to Lillian.

The woman lay on the floor, barely moving and soaking wet.

Before she could even stand, people flooded the chalet.

Police officers. The FBI. Her coworkers from Vanishing Ranch.

It looked like maybe this would finally be over.

Ainsley glanced at Carter again.

He was okay. She was so thankful he was okay.

She wasn't sure what had transpired in that office, but at least he was alive.

That was something she'd forever be grateful for.

———

As soon as the police had Jack in custody, Carter raced to Ainsley and pulled her into a hug.

It had never felt so good to feel her arms around him.

She hugged him back equally as tight.

"Smart move back there," he muttered in her ear.

"Sometimes you have to think outside the box, right?"

He stepped back from her, even though just barely. "That's right. You're okay?"

She nodded and pushed her wet hair out of the way.

"I'm fine. How about you?" She stared at his face before gently touching his jaw.

"It's nothing that won't heal."

"Did Jack get the information?"

Carter shook his head. "I figured out what the key was. But I heard gunfire before I gave it to him. It was perfect timing."

"I'm glad to hear that."

Keeping one arm around each other, they turned to look at the scene.

Puddles filled the lobby area.

A soaking wet Lillian was now handcuffed and scowling at them from across the room.

Hayes, as well as two other guys who'd been introduced as Jesse and Mateo, were here to assist the authorities with anything they might need.

Thankfully, as soon as Hayes had caught wind

that Jack and his cronies were onto him, he'd gone into hiding. But he'd been able to track their movements and follow them up here and alert everyone else as to where they were.

Carter kissed the top of Ainsley's head, thankful that this was over.

Or mostly over, at least.

Jack had been arrested.

Ainsley was safe.

Jason's death had finally seen some justice.

And information his father had wanted to hide hadn't gotten into the hands of the wrong people.

CHAPTER
FIFTY-FOUR

"SO, Jack Earl has been blackmailing people—high powered people—in order to get what he wants and bend things in his favor," Charlie said as she sat at the end of the conference table at Vanishing Ranch for a debrief.

Ainsley and Carter sat beside each other on one side of the table. Charlie's righthand man, Monroe, sat on the other side, as well as a couple other Vanishing Ranch operatives who needed to be in the know.

"I'm guessing Jack started doing this more than fifteen years ago. That he's connected with the Florida bombing, and he had his men set everything up for that." Ainsley's stomach churned at the words.

Jack Earl had killed her brother. Had killed Charlie's grandmother. Had killed Carter's dad.

And all for what? His personal gain?

Ainsley's stomach tightened even more.

"Jack hasn't admitted that yet, but the FBI has a lot of files to dig through," Charlie said. "There's probably evidence there to prove all of this."

"But what if key players in the FBI were paid off to look the other way?" Carter asked. "That's my concern."

As he said the words, he reached under the table and squeezed Ainsley's hand. He seemed to know the inner turmoil she felt, and Ainsley appreciated his empathy.

"It's my concern as well." Charlie frowned, her jaw tightening. "That's why I tried to get more than one agency involved in this investigation. The more people who know, the less likely this can be covered up."

Ainsley shifted in her seat, her eyes narrowed as thoughts churned inside her. "Would Jack have been such a success in business if he hadn't been manipulating people?"

"That's a great question and, as you know, the answer would be pure speculation." Charlie raised her eyebrows. "But my guess is no."

"At least, he'll be behind bars now." Even though Ainsley said the words, they only brought her minimal comfort. Jack Earl had taken innocent lives. Prison seemed too easy a penance.

"This is a small victory." Charlie nodded slowly. "But we're not done yet. I have a feeling other people are involved with this. Other people are pulling strings."

"In other words, we have more work to do." Ainsley leaned back in her chair and sighed.

"Unfortunately, yes." Charlie tapped her pen against the table. "We need to look into exactly who in the FBI was involved. Plus, there's Jack's connection with former President Radar."

"You think it goes up that high?" Carter's voice rose with surprise.

"It's a possibility worth exploring. In the meantime, you deserve a little vacation, Ainsley. Take a week." Charlie's gaze slid between Ainsley and Carter. "Seems like a good idea, yes?"

Ainsley and Carter exchanged a glance.

"I'm okay with that." Ainsley grinned at Carter.

It had only been two days since everything went down. Those two days had been a whirlwind. Ainsley and Carter had hardly had the opportunity to catch up.

But she hoped that might change. They had a lot they needed to discuss.

As Charlie ended the meeting, Ainsley and Carter

stood. Carter took her hand as the two of them headed outside.

Even though it was November, it was beautiful out here in the Arizona desert.

This was where Ainsley felt at home—in wide, open spaces, away from the busyness life seemed to bring.

The two of them strolled into the courtyard out front before pausing.

Ainsley turned toward him. "There's something I've been wanting to tell you."

Carter stepped closer. "What's that?"

She licked her lips. This moment was all she'd been thinking about for the past couple of days. It just felt like it was coming sixteen years too late.

"I love you too, Carter Winslow." Her voice cracked as emotion filled her. "I think I always have."

A slow grin spread across his face, and he lowered his voice as he said, "That makes me very happy to hear."

His lips grazed hers in what seemed to be a promise for more later.

However, right now they still had some other details to figure out.

"So . . . I have a week off." Ainsley stared up at him, not bothering to move away.

Carter tilted his head. "Any idea what you might do with that vacation time?"

She shrugged. "It would be nice if I had someone to spend it with."

"I agree." He pushed a lock of hair out of her face. "Any idea who made your list of people to hang out with?"

She pressed a finger into his chest. "I was hoping it might be you."

The grin tugged harder at his lips. "Me? I like that idea. Where would we go?"

"I was hoping you might go with me to Austin to my parents' ranch. I think Mom and Dad would love to see you. Plus . . . I need to give them an update on the situation." Her smile faltered. "They haven't been the same since Jason died. But maybe some closure will help."

Carter squeezed her arm. "I understand. I'd be honored to go with you."

Relief washed through her. Even though she'd been sure he would agree, the confirmation was comforting. "Thank you."

Before they could talk more, a truck appeared on the horizon. They both turned and watched as a cloud of dust kicked up behind the vehicle. The truck continued closer and closer to Vanishing Ranch.

"Who could that be?" Ainsley muttered as she

stepped away from Carter and braced herself for more trouble. "As far as I know, we're not expecting anyone."

She watched, unable to pull her gaze away. Unable to stop her thoughts from churning. Her instincts from preparing for the worst.

Finally, the truck stopped at the gate.

Ainsley and Carter paced closer. Whoever this was, they didn't have the code to get beyond the fence surrounding this ranch.

She rubbed her arm against the gun holstered at her waist, making sure it was there.

She hoped she didn't have to use it.

A slight man stepped out first—one dressed in khakis and a polo shirt.

As he rounded the front of the vehicle, the passenger door opened.

A girl, probably fourteen years old, stepped out. Based on the girl's defiant gaze, she didn't want to be here. But Ainsley noticed right away that the teen was a head-turner, with her raven-colored hair and refined features.

"Can I help you?" Ainsley called, not opening the gate—not until she knew what was going on.

They didn't have very many unexpected visitors out here. They were so far off the beaten path that the only people who traveled this way were the ones who did so on purpose.

"I'm looking for Charlie Soldier," the man said as he paused beside the girl.

"I'm going to need to know what this is regarding," Ainsley continued, still suspicious.

"I'm afraid that's between me and Ms. Soldier." The man pushed his gold-rimmed glasses up higher on his nose.

He didn't seem like the tough, desert-dwelling type of guy—more like the office type.

So why was he here?

"I'll go get Charlie," Carter offered before jogging toward the main building.

Ainsley remained in place, still on guard.

Her gaze went to the girl again. The teen glanced beyond the fence at the ranch, an unreadable expression on her face.

For some reason, the girl seemed strangely familiar. Yet Ainsley didn't think she'd ever seen her before.

"I'm looking for my mom," the girl said matter-of-factly as she crossed her arms.

Ainsley's eyebrows shot up. "Your mom?"

She frowned. "Charlie Soldier."

The air left Ainsley's lungs. Charlie had a daughter? How was that even possible?

Before Ainsley could say anything else, footsteps sounded behind her. Carter and Charlie headed this way, Monroe with them.

As soon as Ainsley saw Charlie's face, she saw the realization wash over her boss's features.

What the girl had said was true.

Charlie had a daughter.

Why hadn't she ever told anyone?

Based on Monroe's tense expression, he hadn't known either.

Ainsley took a step back, feeling like she shouldn't interrupt this moment. But she also felt as if she needed to be close in case things went south.

"Amberly?" Charlie muttered.

"She needs a place to live," the man said. "I'm Joel, her social worker. Amberly's parents both died in a tragic boating accident a week ago. She was about to go into foster care, but she begged me to bring her here. To you. She was very persuasive."

Emotion filled Charlie's eyes—and Charlie wasn't one to easily get emotional.

But if the girl was that persuasive, it was only another sign she was Charlie's child. Charlie had an amazing way of getting people to do what she wanted. Thankfully, she used that persuasion for good.

Charlie stepped toward the gate, her eyes still on

Amberly as if she couldn't believe what she was seeing.

"She's not going into foster care," Charlie murmured. "Come in. Let's talk."

She pressed a few buttons on the gate, and it slowly swung open.

As it did, Ainsley took Carter's hand and led him to the stables. They would need their privacy right now.

Besides, she and Carter were supposed to go horseback riding.

As they walked away, Ainsley tried not to think about Amberly and Charlie.

But Amberly's sudden arrival was a twist Ainsley hadn't seen coming.

Ainsley gripped Carter's hand, grateful that God had yet again put them in the right time and place to reconcile. She couldn't wait to see what their futures held . . . together.

~~~

Thank you so much for reading *High Stakes Deception*. If you enjoyed the book, please consider leaving a review.

Keep reading for a preview of *Fatal Vendetta*!
~~~

USA TODAY BESTSELLING AUTHOR
CHRISTY BARRITT
Fatal
VENDETTA
VANISHING RANCH VR THE SERIES – BOOK SEVEN

FATAL VENDETTA: CHAPTER ONE

Addison Barlow turned off the lights in her cabin as she stood beside the window. Slowly, she peered around the edge, moving the curtain only by an inch.

She stared at the cabin next door.

The place was probably three hundred feet away. Close enough that she could see it, but far enough away that it was hard to make out any details.

She wasn't trying to be nosy.

But something was going on at her neighbor's place.

Earlier, Addie had met the woman staying there. Brianna was probably in her mid-twenties, and she'd seemed pleasant enough. But something haunted lurked behind the woman's eyes.

Addie recognized the look because she'd lived in that same troubled place before.

Who was she kidding?

She was living there now.

But she couldn't figure out exactly what was wrong. As the two of them had chatted about recipes, Brianna hadn't taken the opportunity to ask for help. But Addie had seen the bruises on her arms.

Just as Addie had gotten back to her cabin, a man in a truck pulled up. He had to be Bruce, Brianna's husband.

Addie had watched as the man climbed from his truck and stormed toward the cabin.

Once inside, the two of them had begun screaming at each other.

Addie couldn't make out the words. But their argument was heated, to say the least.

She'd started to call the police, but she'd stopped herself.

What would she say? Was this a domestic disturbance? Sure, it sounded like the two were having a major disagreement.

But that didn't mean anything criminal was happening. Couples screamed at each other all the time when they fought.

Addie didn't. She'd never again be with a man who yelled at her either.

Eventually, the screams at her neighbor's place had died.

An hour passed, and the argument started again.

Gathering her courage, Addie stepped away from the window and pulled on a coat.

She couldn't stand here and do nothing. She needed to know if she should call the cops or if she was overreacting.

The only way to find out was to get closer. To hear more details.

Remaining in the shadows, Addie crept toward the cabin.

The yelling became louder as she got closer, even though she still couldn't make out any words.

She circled around to the back deck and carefully climbed the old, wooden steps.

A creak sounded beneath her feet.

She paused as fear gripped her.

What would Hayes do if he were here?

Her estranged husband always seemed to know what to do. Decisions came naturally to him. Maybe it was what had made him such a good Homeland Security agent.

That confidence was one reason Addie had been drawn to him. The self-assurance she lacked, he made up for.

They'd balanced each other out.

She bit back a cry as the reality of her loss hit her again.

Hayes was no longer in her life, and she missed him terribly.

Addie needed to get used to doing life without him. Their split had been her choice, and now she needed to live with her decision.

But there was so much more than met the eye to the events that had unfurled . . .

She took another step, and then another until she reached the deck. Remaining low, she crept toward one of the windows where bright, cheery light escaped.

The whole place was an enigma as snow covered the steepled roof and smoke puffed from the chimney. The cabin looked like a cozy storybook picture.

Or maybe the place was more like Hansel and Gretel.

The argument floated outside.

"You don't know what you're talking about!" Brianna shouted.

"And you never listen! Why can't you just listen to me for once? Is it that hard?"

Addie peered around the wall and through the window, trying to remain in the shadows.

Sure enough, the man—Bruce, Addie assumed—and Brianna were quarreling. Bruce leered in Brianna's face. His cheeks were red, and veins bulged at his temples.

The next instant, his thick fingers wrapped around Brianna's arms as he jerked her closer.

"Unless you want to die, you need to listen to me —and listen closely," he muttered.

Addie gasped and reeled back in time as memories of her first marriage pummeled her. Her lungs tightened until she could hardly breathe, and panic claimed her muscles.

Staggering back, her foot hit something.

A bucket.

The metal container clamored to the ground.

She jerked her gaze back to the window.

Bruce had turned toward the sound.

He released Brianna and stormed toward the back door.

Toward Addie.

More fear pulsed through her.

Quickly, she scrambled off the deck and darted away.

Not toward her cabin.

She didn't want to let the man know where she was staying.

Instead, she headed toward the woods surrounding the backside of the lakefront property and ducked behind a juniper. She pressed herself against the tree and waited, praying he wouldn't find her.

Her pulse quickened with fear as the seconds ticked by.

How had she left trouble in one place only to find it here? Was she cursed?

As she peered around the tree, she spotted Bruce. He stalked toward the woods.

Toward her.

Even in the darkness, Addie could see his anger. His motions were stiff and heavy. His eyes narrow. His jaw set.

He paused and glanced around, his hands fisted at his sides.

Maybe he thought the sound was just a raccoon. They had those around here. Even bears visited on occasion. That's what Addie had read in that travel brochure left in her cabin.

She held her breath as she lifted fervent prayers. *Please, Lord. Protect me in my stupidity. Protect Brianna. Help!*

She remembered the verse she'd clung to for so long: *And we know that in all things God works for the good of those who love him, who've been called according to his purpose. Romans 8:28.*

Maybe she didn't love God enough. Maybe that's why nothing in her life ever seemed to work out.

Bruce remained planted at the edge of the woods as he surveyed everything around him.

Addie's heart pounded in her ears.

Maybe she should take this opportunity to run.

But her gut told her to stay put.

She wasn't sure if it was fear or logic that kept her frozen where she was. But she remained still and waited.

Finally, Bruce grunted, turned, and stomped back toward the cabin.

Addie wanted to feel relief—to let the air leave her lungs in a whoosh. But she couldn't.

Especially since she feared Brianna might be in danger.

As soon as Bruce disappeared back inside the cabin, Addie straightened.

Gathering her courage, she sprinted through the woods toward the safety of her cabin.

She had to figure out what to do.

If an innocent woman was suffering at the hands of an abusive man, Addie couldn't simply sit back and do nothing.

She had to help.

But how?

Hayes Barlow gripped the steering wheel of his rented SUV as he drove along the dark, mountainous road.

He hadn't expected the call from Addie.

Hadn't expected to hear the fear in her voice.

And he *definitely* hadn't expected her to ask for his help. Not after the way things had ended between them. Not considering the way she avoided him and wanted nothing to do with him—not even to talk.

But if Addie needed him, there was no way Hayes would say no.

Even if the woman had broken his heart when she'd told him she no longer loved him and that their marriage of nearly two years was done. In fact, their anniversary was in four days. He'd hoped to surprise her with a trip. That was no longer on the table.

He'd given up his job with Homeland Security a few months ago and had started working at a place called Vanishing Ranch. But after Hayes had gotten the call from Addie, he'd informed his boss he needed to attend to some personal business. She'd told him to go.

Thankfully, Hayes had been working a job in Reno, so he wasn't far away from Lake Tahoe—only about an hour. He'd grabbed his things, jumped into the SUV, and taken off.

These roads could be treacherous at any time of

the year. But Hayes knew as he got deeper into the mountains, he'd probably hit some snow. It was late November, and the snow had started falling on and off a month ago.

Still, he had no time to waste.

I think my neighbor . . . she's in trouble. Her husband is hurting her. What should I do?

That's what Addie had told him. Then she'd explained what happened.

Hayes had told Addie to stay in her cabin with the doors locked and not to open them until he got there and asked her to.

He could tell her to call the police, but he was doubtful they'd do anything.

Still, he feared for Addie. She had a big heart. Because of her abusive first husband, Hayes knew that any type of violence shook her up. As it should. As it should *anyone.*

A man should never lay a hand on a woman.

But Hayes's relationship with Addie . . .

He frowned as he gripped the steering wheel harder.

Their relationship was strained, to say the least.

Four months ago, she'd told him she wanted a divorce. Her announcement had come after she'd endured a terrifying home invasion, but Hayes still didn't understand her decision. He'd tried to win her back, to no avail.

That's why Hayes was so surprised she'd called him today.

He wasn't complaining. He'd do whatever it took to win Addie over again.

The road became narrower as he drove deeper into the Sierra Nevada Mountains. He'd come to this area of northeastern California once on a family vacation, but probably twenty years had passed since then.

What was Addie doing out here?

He'd wanted to ask her when she called, but the question didn't seem appropriate considering the gravity of the situation. Besides, maybe it wasn't his business. He was trying to respect her boundaries and give her space, but it was so hard sometimes.

Hayes's GPS showed he was getting close. He took a few more turns until finally his headlights illuminated a small cabin in the distance and the sparkling—but dark—lake beyond.

This place was in the middle of nowhere. Why in the world had Addie chosen this location? It didn't seem like a site a woman would want to travel to alone. The place was so remote Hayes was surprised she'd even had any cell phone service.

He stared at the cabin a moment.

All the lights inside were off, and darkness stared from the windows.

But Addie's car—a white Honda Accord the two of them had purchased together last year—waited out front.

This was definitely the right place.

Quickly, Hayes shut off his engine and climbed out. His gun was holstered at his shoulder, and he'd use it if he needed to.

But he hoped it didn't come down to that.

Glancing at the woods around the cabins, he saw nothing unusual. Yet his nerves were on edge.

Was it because Addie had made it sound as if danger lurked nearby? Or because his instincts somehow sensed the jeopardy around him?

He walked to the front door and gripped the handle.

It was locked.

Good. Addie had done exactly what he'd told her to do.

But, before he talked to her, he wanted to check the outside of this place.

Creeping around the cabin, he paused as his flashlight hit a footprint on the ground.

A footprint that didn't belong to Addie.

It was too big. Too deep. Too rugged.

But the indentation was fresh.

Someone else—a man—had recently been outside this cabin.

Fire raced through Hayes's blood at the thought.

He started back to the front door, now desperate to check on Addie.

But as he stepped around the corner, a shadow lunged at him.

The next instant, everything around him went black.

Click Here to Keep Reading!

COMPLETE BOOK LIST

Squeaky Clean Mysteries:

    #1 Hazardous Duty

    #2 Suspicious Minds

    #2.5 It Came Upon a Midnight Crime (novella)

    #3 Organized Grime

    #4 Dirty Deeds

    #5 The Scum of All Fears

    #6 To Love, Honor and Perish

    #7 Mucky Streak

    #8 Foul Play

    #9 Broom & Gloom

    #10 Dust and Obey

    #11 Thrill Squeaker

    #11.5 Swept Away (novella)

    #12 Cunning Attractions

    #13 Cold Case: Clean Getaway

#14 Cold Case: Clean Sweep

#15 Cold Case: Clean Break

#16 Cleans to an End

While You Were Sweeping, A Riley Thomas Spinoff

The Sierra Files:

#1 Pounced

#2 Hunted

#3 Pranced

#4 Rattled

The Gabby St. Claire Diaries (a Tween Mystery series):

The Curtain Call Caper

The Disappearing Dog Dilemma

The Bungled Bike Burglaries

The Worst Detective Ever

#1 Ready to Fumble

#2 Reign of Error

#3 Safety in Blunders

#4 Join the Flub

#5 Blooper Freak

#6 Flaw Abiding Citizen

#7 Gaffe Out Loud

#8 Joke and Dagger

#9 Wreck the Halls

#10 Glitch and Famous

Raven Remington

Relentless

Holly Anna Paladin Mysteries:

#1 Random Acts of Murder

#2 Random Acts of Deceit

#2.5 Random Acts of Scrooge

#3 Random Acts of Malice

#4 Random Acts of Greed

#5 Random Acts of Fraud

#6 Random Acts of Outrage

#7 Random Acts of Iniquity

Lantern Beach Mysteries

#1 Hidden Currents

#2 Flood Watch

#3 Storm Surge

#4 Dangerous Waters

#5 Perilous Riptide

#6 Deadly Undertow

Lantern Beach Romantic Suspense

Tides of Deception

Shadow of Intrigue

Storm of Doubt
Winds of Danger
Rains of Remorse
Torrents of Fear

Lantern Beach P.D.

On the Lookout
Attempt to Locate
First Degree Murder
Dead on Arrival
Plan of Action

Lantern Beach Escape

Afterglow (a novelette)

Lantern Beach Blackout

Dark Water
Safe Harbor
Ripple Effect
Rising Tide

Lantern Beach Guardians

Hide and Seek
Shock and Awe
Safe and Sound

Lantern Beach Blackout: The New Recruits

Rocco

Axel

Beckett

Gabe

Lantern Beach Mayday

Run Aground

Dead Reckoning

Tipping Point

Lantern Beach Blackout: Danger Rising

Brandon

Dylan

Maddox

Titus

Lantern Beach Christmas

Silent Night

Crime á la Mode

Dead Man's Float

Milkshake Up

Bomb Pop Threat

Banana Split Personalities

Beach Bound Books and Beans Mysteries

Bound by Murder

Bound by Disaster
Bound by Mystery
Bound by Trouble

Vanishing Ranch

Forgotten Secrets
Necessary Risk
Risky Ambition
Deadly Intent
Lethal Betrayal
High Stakes Deception

The Sidekick's Survival Guide

The Art of Eavesdropping
The Perks of Meddling
The Exercise of Interfering
The Practice of Prying
The Skill of Snooping
The Craft of Being Covert

Saltwater Cowboys

Saltwater Cowboy
Breakwater Protector
Cape Corral Keeper
Seagrass Secrets
Driftwood Danger
Unwavering Security

Beach House Mysteries

The Cottage on Ghost Lane

The Inn on Hanging Hill

The House on Dagger Point

School of Hard Rocks Mysteries

The Treble with Murder

Crime Strikes a Chord

Tone Death

Carolina Moon Series

Home Before Dark

Gone By Dark

Wait Until Dark

Light the Dark

Taken By Dark

Suburban Sleuth Mysteries:

Death of the Couch Potato's Wife

Fog Lake Suspense:

Edge of Peril

Margin of Error

Brink of Danger

Line of Duty

Legacy of Lies

Secrets of Shame

Refuge of Redemption

Cape Thomas Series:

Dubiosity

Disillusioned

Distorted

Standalone Romantic Mystery:

The Good Girl

Suspense:

Imperfect

The Wrecking

Sweet Christmas Novella:

Home to Chestnut Grove

Standalone Romantic-Suspense:

Keeping Guard

The Last Target

Race Against Time

Ricochet

Key Witness

Lifeline

High-Stakes Holiday Reunion

Desperate Measures

Hidden Agenda

Mountain Hideaway

Dark Harbor

Shadow of Suspicion

The Baby Assignment

The Cradle Conspiracy

Trained to Defend

Mountain Survival

Dangerous Mountain Rescue

Nonfiction:

Characters in the Kitchen

Changed: True Stories of Finding God through Christian Music (out of print)

The Novel in Me: The Beginner's Guide to Writing and Publishing a Novel (out of print)

ABOUT THE AUTHOR

USA Today has called Christy Barritt's books "scary, funny, passionate, and quirky."

Christy writes both mystery and romantic suspense novels that are clean with underlying messages of faith. Her books have sold more than three million copies and have won the Daphne du Maurier Award for Excellence in Suspense and Mystery, have been twice nominated for the Romantic Times Reviewers' Choice Award, and have finaled for both a Carol Award and Foreword Magazine's Book of the Year.

She is married to her Prince Charming, a man who thinks she's hilarious—but only when she's not trying to be. Christy is a self-proclaimed klutz, an avid music lover who's known for spontaneously bursting into song, and a road trip aficionado.

When she's not working or spending time with her family, she enjoys singing, playing the guitar, and exploring small, unsuspecting towns where people have no idea how accident-prone she is.

Find Christy online at:
www.christybarritt.com
www.facebook.com/christybarritt
www.twitter.com/cbarritt

Sign up for Christy's newsletter to get information on all of her latest releases here: **www.christybarritt. com/newsletter-sign-up/**